Advanced Praise for

"*Sweet & Rough* is the perfect title for t
and passionate erotica that will appea
new readers looking for something h
at night."

—Rachel Kramer Bussel, *The Big Book of Orgasms*

"Sinclair Sexsmith's writing is a surefire panty-wetter."

—Erika Moen, *Oh Joy, Sex Toy*

"So many girls, so little time. Sinclair Sexsmith's new book is the kind of hard-driving, sweet, down and dirty, funny keep-you-on-the-damp-edge-of-your-seat, lovely, filthy erotica you've come to expect from this master of poetry and truth. *Sweet & Rough* will have you on your knees, begging for more."

—D. L. King, editor of *Slave Girls: Erotic Stories of Submission*

"*Sweet & Rough* has been a long time coming. For years, Sinclair Sexsmith immortalized their hottest sexual adventures as erotic stories on Sugarbutch Chronicles, earning a reputation as the Internet's queer Casanova. Writing on BDSM, polyamory, butch/femme (and occasionally my personal favorite, butch/butch) desire, Sexsmith authored the world's largest archive of kinky, queer erotica from a genderqueer, masculine of center perspective. Now edited for our eBook and paperback reading pleasure, *Sweet & Rough* is a rare gift. You'll want to take this one to bed."

—Jiz Lee, *Coming Out Like a Porn Star*

"There are very few erotic writers who consistently capture my attention and admiration. John Preston did. So does Carol Queen. And I've added Sinclair Sexsmith to that list."

—Dr. Charlie Glickman, *Make Sex Easy*

"This is erotica written by someone who has had a LOT of sex."

—Tina Horn, *Love Not Given Lightly*

SWEET & ROUGH

SWEET & ROUGH:
Queer Kink Erotica

Sinclair Sexsmith

Maverick
PRESS

Copyright © 2015 Sinclair Sexsmith

All rights reserved. Except for brief passages quoted in newspaper, magazine, radio, television, or online reviews, no part of this book may be reproduced in any form by any means, electronic or mechanical, including photocpying, recording, or information storage or retrieval systems, without permission in writing from the publisher.

Published in the United States
Maverick Press, 5111 Telegraph Ave #115, Oakland, CA 94609

ISBN: 978-0-9907628-3-6
Library of Congress Control Number: 2015916319
Printed in the United States

Cover design by Mel Reiff Hill of Rowdy Ferret Design, www.rowdyferretdesign.com. Cover image by Cleo Leng via Flickr, used and modified through the Creative Commons 2.0 License. Original at www.flickr.com/photos/skull_bone/4352795205

Some stories in this collection were published in previous anthologies. "One Solid Yellow Aster," *Best Lesbian Erotica 2007*, edited by Tristan Taormino, Cleis Press; "The Diner on the Corner," *Sometimes She Lets Me*, edited by Tristan Taormino, Cleis Press; "Popsicle in the Library" *Afternoon Delight*, edited by Alison Tyler, Cleis Press; "The Worst in Me" previously published as "The Girl in the Red Dress," *Sex Still Spoken Here: The Erotic Reading Circle Anthology*, edited by Jen Cross, Carol Queen, and Amy Butcher, The Center for Sex and Culture Press; "Unlocking," *Love at First Sting*, edited by Alison Tyler, Cleis Press. Excerpt from Toni Amato's story "A Girl Like That" is quoted from *Best Lesbian Bondage Erotica*, edited by Tristan Taormino, Cleis Press.

for my boy

Introduction

Do rough sex fantasies compromise your sex positive ethics?

I firmly believe that there is nothing wrong with my personal rough sex fantasies, nor is there anything wrong with your dirtiest fantasies. I believe that because I trust that you and I are adults who understand that fantasy is different from reality, and while we may think one thing to get ourselves off, we probably conduct our sex lives slightly differently.

Erotic stories are fantasies, yes, but they can be more than just that—they can show us a piece of the path, and encourage our erotic selves to blossom. So what's my responsibility as an erotica writer to make the stories that I write down ethical and responsible?

I am both a sex educator and a smut writer, and sometimes those worlds seem to conflict. For example, in the BDSM and sex education worlds, educators and advanced practitioners stress consent in play scenes. And not just consent—we stress *enthusiastic consent*, not just an absence of "no" but a ready joyous abundance of informed and eager "yes." We also stress safer sex practices, barriers, knowing your status, and sexual health and wellness. We stress responsible scenes, and warn about playing while intoxicated.

In some of my erotic fiction stories, these practices that are deeply held values in my personal life aren't readily apparent. That's because my stories are fantasies—you know, the things you close your eyes and think about when you're getting off all by yourself, not necessarily (though perhaps sometimes!) the things you do with lovers. The characters in my stories sometimes don't negotiate or have a conversation about safer sex, not because things like safer sex or negotiation are unimportant, but because the main purpose of the story is to turn you, the reader, on.

Frequently, in the sexuality education communities and conversations, we talk about how porn and erotica are different from sex education. I discourage people from learning how to give or receive a blow job from porn videos, for example, where deep throating and playing with ejaculate are overly common. (See Cindy Gallop's online project *Make Love, Not Porn* for a variety of other examples of the difference.) Similarly, I discourage people from learning about power dynamics from Laura Antoniou's book *The Marketplace* (though I happen to love the whole series), and would never suggest recreating a scene from *50 Shades of Grey* (don't even get me started). Both of these books are worlds away from the people who pursue and practice power dynamics, ownership, dominance, and submission in their personal relationships.

But the fantasies? We, as readers, love devouring them. We love the fantasies even more than we love the reality. The reality is messy, with STI scares and condoms breaking. The fantasies are escapist, sensual, and by definition *not real*.

I think when we start coming into our own sexually, when we start realizing that there's more to sex than what our completely antiquated and puritanical sex education system taught us as kids, we start familiarizing ourselves with some of the most basic topics in sex positive communities. We learn about consent, agency, negotiations, communication, and safer sex. When we don't see that reflected in the erotica or porn that we are consuming, sometimes it can seem like the erotica or porn fantasy is *discouraging* that kind of sex positive responsibility.

I am explaining all of this to you because I don't want my erotic fantasies to discourage you from being responsible in reality.

I know that the educational workshops I teach encourage sex positive responsibility. But in my erotica? That issue becomes a little more nuanced and complicated, because of the aspects of art and fantasy. For example, I am aware that there are some points in the *Sweet & Rough* collection of stories where characters protest or resist or drink a lot of whiskey. I think there is nothing wrong with playing with resistance and force, consensually and carefully, but I also think that requires a lot of negotiation, a lot of trust, and safewords, in order to be done responsibly in the real world. That part of the story often isn't revealed. Like the porn scene that cuts out the part where the fluffer comes on stage and someone else adds more lube, the erotic story often excludes the getting-to-know-you, the subtle body language communication, the character's histories with each other, and what they have negotiated "off screen."

I deeply believe that the personal is political and that being transparent about one's life is a spiritual path. Since writing *Sweet & Rough*, I have shifted some of my erotica writing to be much more consciously inclusive of things like negotiations and safer sex. Most definitely because that stuff is hot, but also because I want to show more of the reality and less of the fantasy.

However, those things are frequently excluded from *Sweet & Rough*. And here's why: These stories are collaborations. Most of the stories in this collection were written and published on Sugarbutch between 2007-2009. Many of them came out of the "Sugarbutch Star Contest" where readers sent in some basics about a scene (who, where, what the characters did) and I wrote up the story.

It was a huge period of growth for my writing, and I pushed myself hard to write the fantasies that were outlined for me. Sometimes, they were much more forceful than I'd usually write, although they more closely resembled my own private fantasies. I am aware of my access to privilege and unconscious entitlement as a masculine person and as a dominant, and it is important for me to stay conscious in my sex play, especially when it comes to gender or power dynamics.

Often, my early drafts of these stories included a lot of internal processing and negotiations, but the fantasies of my collaborators challenged me. I remember when writing "The Houseboy's Rebellion" (which is a b-side story included on the USB version of *Sweet & Rough*), when the collaborator read the draft of it, she said, "No way. Make my character more mean. Take out all this negotiation. Just *take* me."

Because of how strong the service top in me is, and because I liked it, I followed her desire. And I believe that story—and others, when I received similar feedback—are stronger for it.

The stories in *Sweet & Rough* are fantasies. I know fantasy erotic writing still greatly influences our real sexualities, and I don't dismiss that connection. But these fictions are not necessarily models of sexual responsibility. Some of it is "problematic," and I wouldn't claim otherwise—but they still have so much value, and can jump-start our erotic engines or show us how much more can be incorporated into our erotic lives.

I encourage you to continue practicing being a responsible, ethical, sex-positive kinkster who operates from integrity. And I encourage you to read erotica stories that are edgy, full of force and lust, from authors whose ethics you trust, and to believe that the responsibilities are filled in behind the scenes, just off the page, stripped out so you can enjoy even more of the sweet sex and rough play that gets you going and gets you off.

The Diner on the Corner

As soon as we walk into the diner on the corner, I visualize fucking Shanna on the counter. Or behind the counter, or against to the counter, hell, I don't care—but I am certain the curve of the metal edge, the barstools, and that old-fashioned silver milkshake machine would go perfectly with her rockabilly-femme style.

This is our first date. She picked me up at the dyke bar last weekend while letting me think I was picking her up, and me being enamored with her immaculate femininity—the tattoos on her shoulders, the shade of the pink her nails were painted, the faint flowery scent I wanted to lean into her neck to inhale, the low-cut dress and perfectly curved cleavage, the vibrant hair with streaks of dark purple and red—I didn't notice until halfway through the evening that, though I thought I was warming her up to ask for her number, she was secretly rolling her eyes, thinking, "Get on with it already." She had control of every detail, but let me think I did.

Tonight, I've picked everything out precisely. Black button-down shirt, my favorite sleek red tie, black slacks, solid black freshly-polished shiny wingtips. Plain, simple black fedora on top. Because it may rain tonight.

And because she likes them.

We meet at the movie theatre. She looks incredible: four-inch heels with small straps over the arch of her foot, a little buckle on the side; dark hair down over her shoulders and touching her neck; wearing stockings and a fifties dress that comes just above her knees, slightly flared and layered skirt, low-cut, again, showing off the lovely curves of her breasts. I don't stare. Don't stare, I tell myself. *You're being an asshole.* I try not to stare. *Talk to her face, not her tits.*

"I like your ... hat," she giggles, dark eyes lowered, looking up at me through those lashes, slyly, shyly, from the side, that glance of submission.

I don't blush, but my cheeks get a little warm. "Thanks." I rarely wear hats. I love the way they look, love the tough butchness they play into, but I get self-conscious about what it's doing to my perfectly messy hair—my singular vanity. As soon as we get to our seats, I balance the fedora on my knee and run my fingers through my hair to see how it's holding up. (A little smashed. I try not to care.)

I don't remember the film. Something about music, Dublin, and falling in love. I remember thinking that there should be more sex in it. And that I forget how crowded and bright movie theaters are here in New York City—I miss being able to mess around in the darkest back row.

I do remember the way she laughed, the way she got teary once or twice, the way she kept stealing glances at me. Her hand on my thigh and the—oops—accidental brush against the bulge in my pants. The way her lips circled and sucked the straw in her soda slow.

After the film, we walk to the corner twenty-four hour diner. I slide into the booth and she slides in next to me, stockings on vinyl. Her left thigh touches my right and I feel the brush of her leg against my slacks.

There are a few other diners scattered at tables, but it's late. One old man gumming through chicken fingers and reading the newspaper, and one table of teenagers blowing straw wrappers and eating fries off each other's plates. The waitress comes over and I order a vanilla milkshake and a slice of apple pie, heated. "We'll share," I tell them both.

We chit-chat. I toy with the sugar packets and crunch ice cubes from my water glass. She eases her leg over my thigh, which catches my breath, stirs my cock. I gently put my hand on her knee and let myself finger the thin, silky fabric of her stockings. She's still chatting as if nothing is happening. She liked the film, she's saying. The male lead was cute and sweet in a butch sort of way. "Do you think men can be butch?" she asks me.

My fingers are crushed against her thigh, seeking her creamy skin. I try to pull my consciousness from between her legs to say something intelligent.

"Well, I think that's complicated," I start. "Because ... while I think the gender identities of butch—and femme, too—are inherently queer by definition, I also notice some men with a particularly female flavor of masculinity that is closer to butch than any other word or description ..."

"Yeah!" She has an eager and excited edge to her voice, and presses her leg further into my lap, twisting her torso a little to look more directly at me, opening her thighs. "I know what you mean—but if men begin to have a butch identity, does that invalidate it for the women who have to fight so hard to claim it?"

The layers of her dress are pushing up her thighs and I can feel the edge of her stocking under my fingers, lace and elastic, the line of ribbon up her thigh to her hip: a garter belt. I brush my fingers against the rough edge and press them into her inner thigh, just a little. I wonder how far she'll let me go.

I want to find out how far she'll let me go.

The teenagers clear out and the diner quiets. She leaves her hands on the table, but parts her lips. She's looking at me, gazing at my mouth; I bite my tongue and feel it swell.

Shanna leans in slightly, slowly, ever so subtly, tilting her head without realizing it as my grip on her thigh strengthens. Neither of us notices we do this, we only notice the space between our bodies crackling electrically.

I find the crease of her hip with my fingers, that line where her thighs meet her pelvis.

Her mouth gets closer to mine, inches away. I can feel her breath. She doesn't move any closer but is begging me with her whole body to make a move. To kiss her. To keep moving my fingers up her skirt. She lets me think it's all my idea. She is shifting, something is happening in her body and mind, an intentional submission, an offering up of her mouth and cunt and hungry body. We can both feel it, but it is nearly imperceptible.

"You want ... this okay?" I whisper, fingers getting bolder, brushing against her cunt, the swollen outer labia. I can feel the air between our mouths stirring. The movement of my lips makes them touch hers, briefly, softly. I can nearly see the swirls of her breath, hot and heavy.

She bites her lip at the touch, nods, without moving her head. Submits a little deeper with explicit permission.

"One vanilla milkshake—" the waitress clears her throat and sets it down in front of Shanna, who jumps, but I stay exactly where I am, smiling, amused, then turn my head slowly without moving my hand.

"One apple pie," the waitress sets the small white plate in front of me.

"Thanks," I say, taking a fork with my left hand, my right still between her thighs.

The waitress raises her eyebrows. "You two okay here?"

"Yep," I say. Shanna's cheeks are hot and flushed. She examines the milkshake, stealing a glance at me. My fingers are quiet but persistent, still on the soft of her cunt.

The waitress raises her eyebrows at me again and—I can't quite tell, but—I think she winks. She's cute, the waitress. Dyed black hair, thick tattoo of a faery on her left bicep, those chunky black glasses. She's the only one working, but it's dead in here, so after a round she goes back to reading her book at the counter. She's not paying us any attention.

I twist and shift in the booth and adjust so I can flatten the palm of my hand against her cunt, slowly, cupping it. She's not wearing panties. She knew she could have me. She's controlling every detail.

She inhales and can't look at me, tongues her lip gently. "Are you … will you …" she begins, but can't finish. She wants me to kiss her. I want to ravage her. Thrust her up against the vinyl. Want her hands gripping at the sides of the booth as she comes against my hand.

I grin, that sly cocky grin that says I know what she's asking, I know what she wants, and I'm taking my own damn time giving it to her. She knows she'll get it from me, so my only power here is how and when she'll get it. She offers me her neck and I take it, leaning in, kissing her shoulder, her collarbone, exposed in her low-cut dress. "You have to be quiet," I say. "We're not alone."

"We almost are," she breathes, closing her eyes and tilting her head so I can get to her neck. My fingers run lazy circles around her clit and inner lips, slick already. I dip two fingers inside and feel her muscles pulsing. Slide them in & out while she begins to pant. I circle her clit again, flick it gently and feel her body contract and respond.

"Anybody could walk in," I say. "Anybody could see my hand under your skirt, if they looked for just a second." She shivers and presses her thighs open, presses her cunt against my hand, grips my forearm in one hand. I'm working her clit a little harder, a little faster, and her breathing is coming heavier, her body is tense. She's trying to keep her face still.

"You haven't even touched that shake," I say, nodding toward it. She shoots me a look like she wants to tear me apart with her eyes and attempts to move the tall milkshake glass toward her with one hand. She still wants me to kiss her and I am not letting up with my fingers on her cunt, on her clit, swirling, flicking against the hood, finding that sweet spot where her pelvis tenses and her limbs go limp.

Shanna's eyes don't leave my face as she opens her mouth for the straw and sucks the milkshake into her mouth. Cold. I can see it hit her tongue and explode in creamy sweetness, her eyes roll a little and her pussy responds, presses harder into my hand. She takes another sip and I work two fingers against her clit.

She bends her head back—just a little, just the slightest bit, she wants to be able to throw it back and scream but she can't, she's in a diner, my hand against her, fingers circling, working, flicking, pressing, and her whole body shudders and she grips my forearm in her fist, gasps a little, just a little, and her thighs contract to grip my wrist and she comes, with no sound at all, her body absorbing the noise she wants to make and I don't let up, don't let up at all, until—she gasps, inhales deeply, and pulls on my hand to back off.

I grin and watch her face. She's trying to keep her features together and make it not look like she's just come. Trying to regain her composure. She looks at me a little shyly and embarrassed, unsure about how loud she was, how obvious, and she glances around quickly but there's no one in the diner anymore, the few patrons have all left. It's just us, and the waitress at the counter.

"Holy. Shit," Shanna says softly, still breathing hard. I

still have that stupid grin on my face, that power top grin.

I lean in and kiss her, gently, soft, on the lips. Her mouth is cold and creamy, tastes of vanilla. Sweet. She's a fantastic kisser, all supple and slow. We kiss for a moment and I pull away, still smiling, and she tilts her chin down and looks up at me through her lashes.

"Want some pie?" I ask. I gather a bite on my fork and she nods, I slip it between her lips.

"Oh," she says, chewing, warm apples and cinnamon on her tongue. "It's good. Want some shake?" I take a few sips. It's partly melted now.

The waitress comes over as we are giggling, a little high. "Would you two mind ... ?" She starts. "I'm out of smokes. I'm just gonna run to the corner, be right back."

"Sure," I say. The waitress nods, gives us another quick once-over glance, and spins on her heel. The diner is deserted. It's just me and Shanna. I watch the waitress walk out, the bell on the glass door ringing softly, and turn to look at this gorgeous femme. She's smoothing her hair, already watching me, watching my face, and she slides out of the booth and holds out her hand. I take it and slide out behind her.

"Your turn," she says, crossing the diner floor. Her heels click against the hard linoleum and I watch her ankles as she walks. Her calves, her knees. She keeps her legs tight together, criss-crossing like a model. My mouth waters.

She stops at the counter and raises her arm, guiding me back behind the bar as if we're on the dance floor. I grin and nearly flush, a little embarrassed, flustered to be somewhere I'm not supposed to be, seeing the clutter of dishes, rags, coffee mugs, silverware, napkins, salt and pepper shakers, ketchup and Tabasco bottles. And, of course, the gleaming, polished silver milkshake machine.

I slide behind the counter and she spins on a stool,

crossing her legs at the ankle. She leans over, spilling out of her dress. I lick my lips, run my thumb over them, position myself behind the bar. I grip the handle of the milkshake machine and run my hand over it, stroking.

"So," I say. "Can I get you something?" I'm having trouble keeping my face straight. It feels a little silly, but it's also hot. What will she do? Let me fuck her, here, really?

Shanna purses her lips. "What do you have back there?" She leans over the counter and shifts her hips, then reaches for my belt.

I grab her wrist and hold it for a moment, surprising her. I bring her hand to the package behind my fly and make her feel my hard on. She *ooooh*s a little, still in a character, and lifts her ass onto the counter, swings her legs over it, opening her knees. She grabs my tie and pulls me to her, kissing me hard, running her fingers along the short hairs on the back of my head, wrapping her legs around my waist.

"I want ..." I say between kisses, "I want you, I want you to ... suck me. Would you do that?"

She nods yes and closes her eyes, just for a second, tips her chin down, and slides off the counter. She kisses me again and, palm flat against my cock, fingers on my fly, she unbuckles my belt, unzips, and pulls out my packing strap-on. Swiftly. Expertly.

She kisses me while she does this, hard; she kisses the corner of my mouth, my cheek, my jaw line, my neck, net to my collar, and she sinks to her knees.

The tip of my cock touches her lips and it feels tender, sensitive. As though I can feel her, sucking it into her mouth, working her tongue down the shaft. This is the thrill of the borrowed cock, the filling of it, the way it becomes mine. It is hitting my clit perfectly and her mouth, oh god, her mouth feels exquisite. I want to release into her—want to grab her hair and work her against me, down her throat.

I hold onto the counter instead. The metal edge cuts into my palm. She works her tongue on the underside of the head of my cock and my hips buck, pelvis tightens. I tip my head back, hips forward.

"God," I groan, aware that it is what would give this whole thing away, should someone walk in the door. My expressions. I keep one eye toward the door but my eyelids keep closing. God her mouth feels fantastic.

Shanna looks up at me, eyes wide and shining, cheeks taut, hands on the thighs of my black slacks. I want her, want to fuck her. I look around—where?—we can't have much time, but I already feel close to coming. She sees me glancing around, my stance has changed.

I groan as she sucks me hard, particularly deep, and pull my cock from her mouth. "Wait," I say, "somewhere ... else." I offer my hand and she takes it, rises off her knees back onto her feet.

I have a perfect sightline into the kitchen, and notice the huge walk-in freezer right behind the doorway. There may be people back there, a line cook, a busser, but they wouldn't notice us. We could sneak right in. Shanna sees where I'm looking and waits for me to take a step.

Almost tiptoeing, once I move she follows and we reach the door in a few quick strides. My cock bobs from my fly. I pull on its industrial handle, somewhat thick in my hand and satisfying to grip. I let her go in first.

She turns to face me and brings her shoulders up. "Brrrr." The air is cloudy and it burns my throat a little to inhale.

I survey the situation. A few boxes, milk crates, stacked up in the corner, filled with some heavy containers, jars, lidded plastic. Some of the boxes have been peeled open, others are still wrapped and sealed. Shanna's face reads skepticism.

I sit perched on the edge of the crates and boxes and say, "Come here."

She frowns a little. "What, here? I'm not sure—"

"Oh, hell yes." I stand, take a step toward her, reach out and wrap my arm around her waist. She fits well against me this way. Her arms go up around my neck somewhat instinctively.

"But—" she says, a little too sweetly, batting her lashes at me. She has control of every detail.

"Mmmhmm." I lift her skirt and she gasps at the cold air, it contracts her thighs a little. I take her left knee to the crook of my elbow, and bend my legs to get underneath her, gripping my cock in my fist, sliding inside her slowly but easily. She moans and it is a lovely sound. She's not holding back, begins working her hips against mine, thrusting and circling in s-curves, figure eights. She hooks her foot behind my back and I lean, balancing the weight of our bodies, taking a few steps backward again to lean against the boxes for support. Perfect. Perfect—my shoulders lean and my hips thrust freely, deeper and a little harder, my cock already so hard and her lips are on me, on my neck again, I can see my breath hanging in the air as I exhale, hard, groaning every time she presses against me, and she kisses me, lips full on mine, tongue softly fierce, mouth open, open.

My hands are on her hips. Pressing against her hard. I can feel every place our bodies collide, the heat in such stark contrast to the frigid air. She arches her back and presses me deep, I thrust harder and lose myself in the rhythm, hard, and again, again, against her as my muscles contract, face tenses, pelvis thighs ass tense, hard, harder ... and then shuddering release, still thrusting and vibrating against her, getting softer, slower, coming down.

I hold onto her and breathe into her neck, her hair, for a moment. We kiss, giggle, weave that sex haze, gather ourselves.

Shanna exits the freezer first and returns to our table, and I follow. I pull my wallet out of my back pocket and the bell on the door jingles, the waitress tosses her cigarette into the street after she's opened the door and then turns to see me tossing a few bills onto the table.

I pick my fedora up from the table and set it onto my head, run my fingertip over the rim, and slide my wallet back into my pocket. Shanna has one knee on the vinyl booth and takes another mouthful of vanilla milkshake.

"C'mon, doll," I say, offering my hand. She takes it and the sound of the milkshake glass hitting the table echoes. "Let's blow this joint."

She laughs. I'm being a bit ridiculous. Ah well, why not? I circle my arm around her waist, wink over my shoulder at the waitress, and we walk out of the diner on the corner.

Unlocking

"What's this key for?" Maya asks, fingering the smallest key on the keychain clipped to my belt loop. I toss back the last mouthful of whiskey, now watered down from the melted ice.

"It's a handcuff key," I say, watching her face for a reaction.

"Really," she says. Her wide brown eyes flash gold and reveal her desire. "I've never been handcuffed before."

I don't miss that invitation. "Would you like to be?"

Her hips switch and tilt. Oh yeah, she wants to be. Possibly even by me. "I don't know," she says slowly, placing herself closer to me with every imperceptible movement. Her fingers are still in my belt loop and she's pulling at the circle around my hips. I'm leaning back into it and making her lean into me. She tilts her face up toward mine, a good four inches shorter than my not-so-tall five foot six, and does that doe-eyed under-the-eyelashes look of girls who want to be kissed.

I reach behind her to set my glass on the tall table near the jukebox, changing places with her. She turns too, and now her back is to the wall. She leans against it and hooks both thumbs into her pockets, holding her bottle of Corona by the neck in her left hand. Only the lime at the bottom is left.

I take the bottle out of her hand and use that as an opportunity to touch her skin. I pass the bottle to my other hand and set it on the table next to my empty glass, barely looking to see where it lands, eyes locked on Maya's dark, thick eyelashes and smoky makeup. She's biting her lip. I have the back of her hand in mine and press her palm with my thumb. Her fingers are a little colder than her wrist. It's a little cool out on the back patio tonight, but we're both beginning to sweat.

My thumb and forefinger circles her wrist and I squeeze, just a little, enough pressure to let her feel restricted. I take her other hand, notice that she's already reaching for me, and do the same. She breathes in, a little surprised at the sudden movement. I press her wrists back until they touch the wall and see the tension in her shoulders. Her breasts are offered up to me like fruit to suck on in order to bring out the flavor of the whiskey and she knows it; she sees me considering her and arches further. I want to press my palm into the ripeness of her chest and feel the flesh pushed between my palm and the wall. I want to take a bite of the taut muscles of her neck. I want to run my tongue from her chin down past the collar of her thin cotton blouse and into the V of her neckline where she has one too many buttons undone.

I don't do any of these. I keep my eyes on her face as she tells me what she wants, what she's afraid to give away, what she wishes I'd keep doing to her, without saying anything.

Maya's mouth makes a sweet, high whimper that is quickly cut off by my own mouth pressing into hers. She pushes her hips into mine and made a move in to kiss me that was more sudden than I expected, and I almost lose my balance and my grip around her wrists. I pull her hands behind her back and they touch easily; her wrists are thin enough to get both locked in one of my hands, so I bring my left hand to the back of her neck, along her spine and under her long dark hair. Her body arches and she kisses me harder, her tongue beginning to feather my lips. I open my mouth, catch her swollen bottom lip between my teeth gently, then pull away and touch her lips as lightly as possible. She's pressing toward me for more but I'm holding her back by her wrists. She struggles against my grip and almost gets one wrist free before I catch it in my left hand. She smiles against my mouth, I feel the corners of her mouth turned up and laughing. She flexes her fingers and stops struggling.

I pull back and she's still smiling. I let go and she brings her hands between us, touches one wrist with the other, then pulls on my keys again.

"Take me home with you," she says. I grin. Circling her right wrist with my left hand, I lead her back through the pulsing bodies on the dance floor, and out the front door of the bar.

*

I get nervous when we arrive at my small studio apartment, like I always do. I start over-thinking things and worrying that I'm not being enough of a host, that I don't even know this girl, that I'd misread her. She gazes at the simply framed black and white nude portrait photographs on the walls, her hands cupped behind her back like she's wandering through a museum. Or as though she is offering her wrists to me to bind.

Rustling through the small wooden chest next to my

bed, I come up behind her, my face in her hair, she smells amazing, some musky-floral scent from her crème rinse or perfume, and I push her hands in front her of with my thumbs and first fingers in an L shape. She catches sight of the cuffs dangling from my fingertips and touches them lightly, turning the leather over in her hand, feeling the metal clasp and chain that links the two loops of leather together.

"My best friend's a photographer," I say, my arms around her as I open one cuff in each of my hands as an invitation. "She always gives me photos as gifts. These are my favorites." My lips are touching her ear as I speak, then the line of her jaw, then her neck.

She sighs and slips her wrists into the cuffs one at a time as I keep them stable. "I like this one," she says, indicating an abstract close up of a neck and shoulder blade, her back arching again, turning her head a little. She wants to kiss me. I can see her lips part, her breath getting shallow and quicker.

I snap the cuffs closed with the thin sound of metal on metal. "They'll stay closed without being locked," I say, "but if you pull them apart, hard, they'll open."

She considers this. I want her to have the option of a quick out, in case she has a moment of panic. They will still hold in place through quite a bit of pressure and pulling, and she tests this by pulling her wrists apart slightly. They don't open.

"Will you lock them?" she says in a small voice, turning to face me but keeping her eyes low. She has such submissive instincts. This is going to be beautiful.

I let out a rush of air that I didn't realize I was holding in, and swallow. I unclip my keys from my belt loop and take the small silver key between my fingers. I hold her hands up between us and watch her face as I lock each wrist closed, then clip the keys back onto my jeans. She raises her arms up and I circle her tiny waist with my arms while she settles her hands behind my head, forearms on my shoulders. Our mouths meet again and it is sweet, tender, hungry. She presses against me hard and my keys dig into the bone of my hip. She's on her toes to reach me and wants to bring her legs around my waist, I can tell by the way her hips are opening and how she easily, eagerly lets me lift her thigh with the slightest touch of my hand as her knee bends and the small heel of her sandal finds the back of my knee.

Taking a few steps backward, I pull Maya along with me until we are next to the small tan couch against the wall. I sit back and she bends from the waist, then moves one leg at a time to either side of my hips, kneeling over me, placing her hands, still restrained, behind my head. Our faces are close and her hair is falling in her eyes; I push it behind her ears with my fingers, then trace the line of her blouse down to its first button, three of them already unbuttoned, slipping it through its buttonhole. She kisses me. I am beginning to identify the taste of her mouth, behind the lime and Corona, as the essence of a summer night, the kind after a long day outside in the sun. She tastes like the night air in summer when it's about to turn fall and the trees are beginning to shiver their leaves. I still taste like whiskey.

Her hips are working up and down on mine like we are already fucking, like I am already inside her, like I have a cock inside my jeans and she is ready to milk it till I come.

I get her blouse undone but of course it won't come off over the cuffs, so I just slip it off her shoulders and it catches at her elbows, which further restricts her arm movement and frames her collarbone, cleavage, and light pink bra nicely. Her breasts are smallish, the bra is more for shape than support (unlike my own), but are comfortable handfuls and a lovely round, full shape. Her nipples are hard, her areoles already wrinkled. Maya's skin starts to sheen with sweat. My lust is building strong, my clothes are getting tight. I want to take my lips to her nipples. I want to see her breasts bound with rope.

Maneuvering her onto her back on the couch, I twist and set the weight of my body between her legs as she presses her hips up to meet me. My keys are still sharp against my hip and they may be scratching the exposed skin of her stomach. I bring a hand up to hold the cuffs above her head and her back arches, she inhales, her stomach tightens.

"Oh god, you feel so good," she whispers through the thickness of her desire, when I lower my mouth to her breastbone and push her bra off of her darkening nipple. It contracts in my mouth and I work it like a clit, flicking it with my tongue fast then lapping in broad strokes. She presses her hips into me and moans.

"Can I take your jeans off?" I say quietly, letting go of her wrists to tug at the waist of her jeans. She nods.

I pull them off easily, revealing tiny cream-colored panties, satin and thin, and leave them on. I pull my own black tee shirt over my head to reveal a very plain black binder. She sits up, intending to take it off of me, but can't reach her bound hands around me to get to the clasp. She realizes this quickly.

I indicate her wrists. "Do you like those?" I ask.

She nods, a little embarrassed by her own submission. "Yes," she says. She pulls at my keys, touches my stomach. I step up off the couch and go back to the toy box.

"I have some rope," I say. "Can I bind you? Tie you up?" I can feel the questions in her face with my back turned. What would I bind? Her wrists, her ankles? Would she like it? Would I fuck her while she was bound, or after?

From the toy box I remove two twelve-foot lengths of black rope, wrapped in neat bundles. Maya is sitting up on the couch, white blouse pulled down around her elbows, wrists in her lap. I set one of the ropes on the bed and bring the other over to her. In a flourish of movement designed to look impressive, I shake the rope free from its bundle. She watches me as I kneel on the wood floor in front of her, between her legs.

We are nearly eye to eye this way. I set the rope on the couch and unclick my key ring. I touch her hands, lightly running my fingers over her soft skin, and she shivers. Her hands are more sensitive and responsive than she realizes, and it catches her off guard. They have become a new erogenous zone. She closes her eyes for the sensation.

I lick my lips. "Are you ready?"

She nods. I sit back on my heels and unlock the cuffs one at a time, then set the keys aside and take each of her hands in mine, kissing the tendons of her wrists, the bones in her fingers, her swirled fingerprints. I raise to my knees and she reaches for me, we kiss again, she melts against me, trusting my grip on her and giving me a serious hard-on by wrapping her legs around my waist again, pulling me back. I get hold of the thin, soft fabric of her white blouse and manage to remove it, along with her bra. She pulls at the rope next to her, tangles her hand in it, feels it between her fingers, then hands it to me.

"What are you going to do to me?" she asks, barely breathing, eyes wide and begging for it, whatever it is, she doesn't even know, but she hopes it involves her getting tied up and fucked, she didn't even know she wanted that until tonight, until right now. I can see her desire like a string of Braille in the air between us, carefully placed for me to decipher.

I stand up and pull her to her feet. I drape the length of rope over her shoulder and drag it along her bare skin. The sensation, the movement, is tiny, but so specific that every nerve in her skin feels it.

"First, I'm going to bind your breasts in a chest harness, which will look like an X across your chest and will increase the sensitivity of your shoulders." I kiss the top of her shoulder. "And your breasts," my mouth moves to the arc where her breast meets her clavicle. "And your nipples," I roll one nipple in between my fingers as I continue to slowly drag the rope over her stomach.

"Then, if you want it, I'm going to bind you here," I say, gently aiming the friction of the rope between her thighs, letting it graze the fabric of her panties and her swelling cunt. "If you want it," I say again.

"I want it," she whispers, nearly whimpering, "Yes, I want it," she adds, to be sure I am clear. Her eyes are closed and she's keeping her breathing low and even. The urge to lunge for me is clear, she's never felt this slow agony before and she thinks she likes it. She doesn't want it to end and she wants more, wants to feel it all over, wants to feel her muscles pull against restraints again.

I smile. "Good. Hold this here," I say, finding the thin red ribbon tied to indicate the midpoint of the rope and placing it right between her breasts. "Just for a minute while I start the binding." I fight the urge to toss the rope on the floor and kiss her, hold her, fuck her, feel the muscles of her cunt and watch her face as I make her come.

Maya keeps the midpoint between her breasts, and I drape the ends over her shoulders, wrapping them under her arms and under her breasts, crossing the ends under the loop of the midpoint. She watches me in the heavy mirror hanging on one wall, near the room's only closet, watching me weave the rope around her small breasts, criss-crossing, until it curls around her like ivy, finding every possible place to cling. Then I'm done, she's bound; I stand back to admire my work.

"How does that feel?" I ask, running two fingers

between the rope and her skin, testing the tension.

She breathes out and closes her eyes. "Good."

"Not too tight?" I say.

She considers. "No."

"Breathe in deep. Make your lungs full," I say. She does. The rope barely constricts her, only just at the end of the inhale. I smile. "Lovely."

"It's … good," she says again, already near panting, turned on, sipping hard at the air around her as her chest expands and contracts. Her eyes are sheened with diamonds, sparkling, her face upturned to me and opening, wanting. Her body's sensitivity is already heightened; she's waiting for me to touch her.

My hands don't leave the ropes. I continue to run two fingers between the ropes and her skin, one hand on her lower back so she can use me for support. Her skin is creamy caramel, fine as-sandy beaches and I feel as though I could dip my fingers inside, pull out tiny shining treasures. She ripples under my touch.

"You look beautiful," I say, lowering my mouth to suck on her shoulder, her neck, her collarbone. She leans into me and moans. I stand behind her, wrapping my arms around her, cupping her breasts in my palms and rolling her nipples in my fingers, touching my lips to my skin everywhere I can reach.

"You feel amazing," she says, her breath part air and part moan. "So amazing. My skin is so alive."

"One more length of rope, and you can relax," I offer, moving to the bed to retrieve my second twelve-foot length of rope. Maya follows, keeping the distance between us close.

I position myself behind her again, gently peeling her cream-colored panties off of the perfect roundness of her ass cheeks, making my hips twitch and my internal cock harden; my desire is hard to manage. I want to feel her long, slender fingers on the shaft of my strap-on, want to watch her ride my hips, want to feel myself thrusting inside her. I want her mouth on my fingers, on my clit. I try to fight the raw urges and begin to bind her again, quicker this time. I run my fingers over her smooth belly, over her hips and thighs, careful to avoid her cunt; I want to wait until we can't wait any longer.

I find the midpoint of the second rope and grip it in my palm, folded. I press her legs apart with my knees and her knees begin to buckle, but she strengthens her legs and spreads, wide, instead. I press my hand between her legs, still avoiding touching her cunt, and thread the rope through to my left hand in front of her.

"Will you hold this, here, please?" I ask, pressing a tiny bit on the midpoint, now placed at the top of her pubic hair, to indicate where to hold the rope. Her hair is trimmed and neatly edged, thick though, and dark, like the hair on her head. I try not to imagine what she'll taste like, how she'll move and moan, how she'll let me take her, how far in she'll let me go.

She holds the rope in place and I gently trace the rope with my fingers as it disappears between her legs, between her labia, finding her hole wet, dripping, slicking the rope immediately, swollen with want. I kneel and trace my fingers alongside the rope, gently tickling her labia this time with my fingertips, pulling the folds of her out of the way and placing the slim rope just where I want it: parting her slick lips and opening her for the taking.

She is quiet, controlling her desire with even breaths. I wrap each of the two ends of the rope around each hip, then under the midpoint she's holding, waiting. The ends pull the small amount of slack in the rope taut and pull open her labia further, making a triangle out of the rope, mirroring the triangle of hair between her legs. Each end of rope then runs behind her back laid over her hips, crossed at the small of her back, and tied in front, a few inches below the rope binding her breasts, and just above her belly button.

I test the rope's tightness again, pulling on the line across her hips, then at her cunt, slipping my fingers between her legs. She's so soft and tender, so trusting, and she doesn't really even know me. It's beautiful and touching that I could be so trustworthy, that I could be handed the power to control, to invade, to be inside of this gorgeous creature, open before me. I want to feel every inch of her skin. I can't wait, the knots are tied, the rope is on, she's mine, she's offering up the most secret places she has; I have to take her. I circle the opening of her hole with my fingers, slip one inside her with no effort, and add another. She shudders against me, gasping.

"Yes—" she whispers, barely audible. "Oh yes, do that, more, again." My mouth waters. She grips my hand, the one that's inside her. I kiss her, hard, slide another finger inside and slowly move them in and out, curling my knuckles to massage the walls of her cunt. Her mouth is greedy and she sucks my tongue, bites my lip, opens wide to let me taste her. She presses her body to mine and the ropes are hard, a little surprising, biting into the skin of my stomach.

"Oh god, fuck me, yes do that—there—" She's close to coming already, her cunt contracting around my fingers and pulling them deeper inside of her. I manage to get her to the bed and lay her down. She brings one arm overhead immediately and grips the headboard, keeping one hand on mine which is still inside her, touching her clit with her fingers. She moans, closes her eyes, her face open mouth open cunt open palms of her hands open and she's gasping, breathing hard, noises coming from the back of her throat where the air is escaping through muscles contracting, opening everywhere. She takes my fingers in deeper and I can feel everything, every rippling muscle. Her stomach contracts and pulls at her breasts, shimmering, her nipples hard and darkened. I catch one with my mouth. Flick it with my tongue and suck. Her fingers are working her clit and I'd like to watch but it's not about me, it's about her body now, about how she's telling me to open her creases, her corners, her locked boxes.

Maya comes, grasping, growling, pushing her cunt into my hand, hard, as her thighs jerk back, knees bent and angled, pulling her body into a fetal crunch, stomach contracting, muscles pulling and releasing over and over until she's moaning, nearly whimpering, chest heaving against the ropes, hips wide and pressed to the bed, eyes still closed. She quiets and I leave my mouth on her skin, my tongue on the spaces where the ropes criss-cross the tightest, press my body thick and warm next to hers and she curls around me, presses into my jeans, my chest, drapes her fingertips over the skin of my back and neck, across the shortest hair on the back of my head. My fingers find the rope knotted under her breasts, on her stomach, and I work them loose, pulling slack into the tight bindings. She sighs, nuzzles a little into me, smiles into my neck.

*

Later, after she is untangled and has pulled her tiny cream-colored satin panties back on, her jeans, her light pink bra, her white blouse, sandals on her delicate feet, she looks at me again with those doe-eyes, that look not just like she wants me to kiss her but that she wants me to keep kissing her, tomorrow, next week, in her bed, in the park, when she steps out of a car. But I don't really know anything about this girl, and she doesn't know me. She wants to ask to see me again, but swallows the words and the flavor of my whiskey in the back of her throat instead.

Maya leaves a scrap of paper on the top of my dresser that reads *Next time I'm in charge. Maya 212-271-7201*, with loops on the *n* and the *m*. On her tiptoes in the doorway she kisses me, tilts her face up toward mine, those impossibly wide brown eyes soft and golden, shining, clear. She looks shy for a moment, then asks, "This is going to sound terrible, but … what's your name again?"

"Sinclair," I say. "My name's Sinclair."

One Solid Yellow Aster

I knock on the door and wait. Five flights up to the run-down Chinatown loft and they're not even home. Great. I knock again. Finally, a girl answers the door wearing nothing but a thin white robe, somewhat sheer, dripping off of one shoulder. It looks silky, soft. She may have nothing underneath. It covers her knees but is loosely tied, generously gaping at her thighs. I don't stare. I try not to think about how cliché this is. Her eyes light up at the sight of me, my black-and-white delivery uniform, the huge bouquet of spring wildflowers cradled in one arm. Ten stems of larkspur, seven blue iris, and one solid yellow aster, accented with "lush greenery and festive purple-tinted foliage." One of the more popular deliveries now that it's spring. Pretty, but not a lot of imagination, which is unfortunate; this girl clearly deserves something unique.

She looks familiar, actually, but I can't place her face. Maybe I've slept with her before.

"Delivery," I say, looking down at the well-organized list on the clipboard in my other hand. "For Rachel ..." I recognize her last name and suddenly struggle with it.

"That's me," she says, leaning slightly against the

hallway just inside the door, an amused smile on her face. "What, you don't remember me, Sinclair?"

"No, I do, I'm sorry, I uh ... you cut your hair," I try to justify.

She fingers the back of her neck. "For a play, a few months ago. It's growing out. Taking a lot of getting used to. Are those seriously for me?" she asks, eyes on the iris.

"Just sign here." I offer the clipboard, then hand over the vase.

We stand awkwardly for a moment, then she says, "Come in, have a glass of something."

"I can't, I ..." But before I can answer she's already turned, walking down the hallway, readying the flowers for display. She leaves the door open and doesn't look back to see if I'm following; she knows I will.

"I didn't know you moved to Manhattan," I start. "Last I knew you were in Queens, with ... what's her name?"

Rachel rolls her eyes. "Alexis. Don't remind me; that was a mess. Well, I'm here now. Who sent the flowers?" she asks, smoothly maneuvering the conversation in that way she always could.

I check the clipboard. No name. We tend not to allow that, actually; too many weirdos. She's examining the bouquet: no card. I wonder if it was Alexis. I wonder how long ago they broke up. "Don't know," I say. "No name. Your girlfriend, boyfriend, one-night stand from last night maybe?"

Rachel rolls her eyes visibly. "Not possible," she says airily, running the stems under water as she slices them and puts them back in the vase in some particular Rachel order. I lean against the counter. "I'm not seeing anyone anymore. They aren't from you, are they? Some far-fetched attempt to get back with me?"

"We were never together," I remind her. "But no, they

aren't from me. I didn't even know you lived here."

"We should've been together," she purrs, leaving the flowers and moving close to me, closer, a little too close. She's going to kiss me or grab the waist of my jeans any second. "You know it. Are you sure it wasn't you? You always were so *bold* with me."

Her hair smells like girl product, flowery and fruity. I notice it's a little damp. "Did I interrupt you?" I ask, touching the tie of her robe that would unknot with the gentlest tug.

"I was in the bath," Rachel says, turning back to the flowers, twisting a few stems, fingering the petals. She picks up the vase and moves to the cream-colored couch—the two rooms connected and open—setting them on the end table, and calls, "So, you still single?"

I swallow. "Actually, yes. Actually, I'm not even really sleeping with anybody these days. It's been a while."

She looks at me questioningly, eyebrows raised. "Really. That's different, for you. Well, me too," she offers. She settles onto the couch, pulls her knees up underneath her, pats the cushion next to her. "I miss not being with someone, but it's kind of nice to have time to myself."

"I think what I miss most is the kissing," I say, settling down, getting into it. "Really deep, or light, or whatever, just lots of kissing." And her mouth is so fucking pretty. It's hard not to think of kissing.

"Yeah, I miss the kissing. And I miss light touching , the kind that almost tickles."

"Yeah, I love that," I answer. "Especially after."

"Yes," she says, breathes in. "After."

Her lips curl and part and I can almost see her warm breath moving between them. I try not to stare. "I love it when you smile like that," I say quietly.

She doesn't really hear me, or maybe she does, but keeps going. "I tend to want to hold on to the person I'm with after. Lots of silence and breathing." Her eyes soften.

"I love that. That closeness can be so intense, and beautiful. When you feel like your bodies are so close and connected. It can be amazing."

"You know what else I miss?" Her voice gets anxious, faster. "The intense feeling of being wanted, the before. The moment when you suddenly feel so wanted, so sexy, from the energy coming off of the other person."

"Yeah, I miss the wanting," I agree. "I always feel so transparent. I always think I'm hiding it, but I wear my emotions so obviously."

"Oh, me too. I become bold in certain instances, though. I start saying what I'm thinking out loud. I stop being embarrassed." Rachel's eyes shine playfully.

I'm still thinking about her kissing comment, and her mouth, her skin, her taste. Kissing everywhere. "Kissing is so similar to going down on a girl, too, which I also just love, and miss."

"Jesus ..." she says, almost under her breath. Her body flutters a little, which is exactly what I wanted. "I haven't had the pleasure of doing that in over a year." She says. "I haven't done it that much, but I miss it, a lot actually. It seems I miss a lot of things."

"Yeah, there's a lot to miss." I pause, then continue, absently brushing my hand against her knee, exposed through a gap in her robe. She watches my fingers. "I love that moment when it turns from kissing to sex."

She leans her head back just slightly. "That moment when a hand slips under your shirt just slightly. Like it's asking for permission. And then when your body gives it, by pushing back just so."

"I miss the throw-down, the taking control. I love that feeling, when I have permission to do it." I'm feeling bold. She always could do this to me.

"And I love surrendering. In that sudden, amazing moment where I feel completely taken care of … so I no longer need control. Control is so vital for me in most of my life, so when I'm able to give it up, it's so thrilling."

"I miss having someone trust me like that." I stop again. Something occurs to me, and I smile. She's caught. "Are you trying to seduce me?"

"What," she says, eyes sparkling, "am I not making it obvious enough?"

She moves toward me, as if to straddle me, but I move to push her down onto the couch at the same moment and instead, neither of us go anywhere. I get caught up, ahead of myself, and shy all at once. But it's her, Rachel, my Rachel, the girl I used to dance with every weekend at Meow Mix, who I used to run into everywhere, who I used to fantasize about while getting off with someone else. Something about her hips, the perfect roundness of her breasts, her fucking perfect mouth. I've wanted her for so long. Shit. I laugh, mostly at myself, softly, to cover up the desire. "Why do I feel so …? I've had a crush on you since—when? Ninety-seven?"

"Ninety-eight. And it's mutual," she says, gazing at me with that seductive Rachel look. "Don't be shy."

I run my fingers along her cheek, then her jaw, to the back of her neck where her short hair is still a surprise. "A long time."

"Yes," she says. "A long time." Damn, she is on. I breathe and clear my throat again. Nervous. I look around her new place and admire her music posters, theatre posters, delicate decorations. The early afternoon sun creeps through her windows and the airy orange-yellow curtains paint pastel tones through the open rooms. Most of her shelves and walls are still bare, and small stacks of boxes are tucked in between the furniture.

"How long have you been at this place?" I ask.

She stiffens a little, but doesn't falter. "More than a month," she says. "It's starting to feel like home, but I haven't even unpacked my vibrator yet. Isn't that awful? It's not lost," she corrects herself. "It's just hiding out. It's been six months I think. I've lost my drive entirely."

I glance at her sideways. "You should unpack it."

"I should unpack it, huh? So it can sit in the nightstand." She sighs dramatically. "This conversation has depressed me. Lord, and you always said that I was the tease."

"I'm not trying to depress you, rather the opposite—to inspire."

"Well. Yes." She presses up against me, lowers her voice, lowers her eyes, lowers her hand to my crotch, attempting to be subtle and still obviously checking to see if I'm packing. "Do that. Inspire me. Please?"

"You really haven't had sex in six months?"

She recalculates. "Seven," she says, certain this time. "Seven months."

I clear my throat, swallow. There is little more that I would rather do than spend the afternoon in bed with this beautiful girl. But I'm so loaded down with deliveries today, and there's been nobody but the one girl for two years. Will I even remember how to do this?

"Rach, I have to go, I have more deliveries, a full schedule this afternoon."

"Yeah I know, I have work to do too. I'm supposed to be at the theatre in half an hour. But, I just want you to tell me more."

I look at the clock on my cell phone and gauge my afternoon, counting the minutes in my head. I see her watching me. "Fifteen minutes," I offer. I can't just leave, not with her all smooth and bare and begging on the couch next to me like this. "We'll see how far I can get."

"Yes," she nods, and kisses me, gives herself over, her mouth like a ritual offering. Warm, soft. She's already making those little *oh*s and *mm*s from her throat.

I don't waste any time. I pull her robe from her shoulders and press my hands inside, touching her skin, her beautiful curves.

"Bedroom," I say, an order and a question. She moves her tongue over her lips where I've pulled away, her body thick and wanting, then stands and leads me. Her robe is falling off of her everywhere and she doesn't stop to adjust it.

Her bedroom is set up in an elaborate romantic scene of lit candles and slow music, with soft blankets on the bed. It's darker than the living room because the curtains are thick, but there's still some daylight trickling through. I wonder if I had been expected. If she'd known I was going to come. I slip the robe to the floor and lay her down naked, taking my time, slow, excruciatingly slow, lying next to her, kissing, hands everywhere.

She pulls on my black pants, my button-down white shirt that seems strangely formal next to her naked skin. She's trying to rush me, wants me up in her, wants me exploding in her, wants me everywhere all at once. I notice massage oil on the nightstand. No vibrator, but oil. I imagine her in here after her bath, skin supple and puckered from soaking too long, slathering oil along her freshly shaved legs, hands, elbows, breasts. Sitting alone with the oil on her skin.

I pick it up and rub my hands with it, put my hands on her belly, her legs, her hips.

"Why would you make me wait, after all this time, huh?" Her eyes flash, she's curious and frustrated and desperate all at once.

"Because I can," I say. "Because you're looking at me with all that want. I can feel it from here."

"So what, you're going to torture me?"

"Maybe not entirely. And you'd like that, anyway." I see right through her.

She breathes in, sighs. "You know me too well."

I keep going, lovely soft touches, lots of kissing. She tries to get to my buttons, the seam of my pants, and I have to grab her wrists every once in a while, set her arms above her head, hold them to her sides.

"I can be pretty good at doing what I'm told," Rachel whispers. "Just ask."

"I want to touch you," I say. "I want to see if you can just lie back quietly and feel me, without moving, without responding. Just lie back and feel me." I feel her relax, and run my hands over her skin, run my fingers along her legs and arms; her sides, a little ticklish; her back; her stomach. She tries to stay still, she does, but it's hard for her not to move. Her back has a tendency to arch at will. It's beautiful. I can hear her breathing deepen, grow heavier. Her skin is all honey and smooth, sweet and dimpled, freckled in places, contoured perfectly. I don't know how many times I've been up against her begging for this to happen, don't know how many times I've been at home alone wishing for this skin to be under my hands. I maneuver my body above hers, between her legs, softly; she opens quickly and her hips curl, knees bend. I hold myself up by my arms, not really touching her, watching her eyes, her skin as she flushes and struggles for control over her desire.

I kiss her, soft and deep, and let some of my weight fall on top of her. She has trouble keeping quiet. Whispers and sighs and moans.

I feather my fingers over her chest, trace her breasts, barely touch her nipples. "You're so beautiful," I whisper. It takes restraint not to press inside her, hard, not to fuck her now.

She whimpers a little. "This is hard," she says. "I'm really trying not to just ... open my legs so you can feel me."

"I could get used to this view of you, naked under me like this," I say. She's open, so open. All blushing and wanting.

She circles her hips and tries to remember that I asked her to be still. "I have wanted you to fuck me for a very long time," she says slowly, choosing her words deliberately, making sure I hear every single one and all she's not saying in between.

I start with my fingers, just barely touching her thighs, the creases at her hips, her stomach; touching the hair between her legs but only so she can feel where my fingers are. I kiss her, soft, slow; moving against her, agonizingly tender. I move the other hand to her hair, so short now, and stroke the back of her neck.

She starts pressing up into me. "I want you."

I pause, smile into her neck, kissing, nibbling gently. "Yeah? How much?"

She moans. "So much," she offers. "I haven't felt like this in so long. You're softer than I imagined you'd be."

I harden temporarily. "I don't have to be soft," I say, almost defensively.

"I know you don't. I can't stop thinking about how you'll feel inside me. Please, I want to feel you, I can't wait. I don't know how much longer I can keep still." Her eyes are pleading, her lips parting. Her skin is amazing, all cream and sugar. I'm sure the folds of her are, too. It's so pale in places, stretched taut over muscle and curves, I sometimes expect to be able to see through it. My fingers are still between her legs, giving feathery touches, teasing. I slowly, slowly start letting my touch get firmer, cupping her cunt with my palm, feeling the heat of her in my hand.

"I'm asking you to," I say again. "Just a little longer. I know you want to please me."

She breathes and her body quiets. "Yes." She focuses on my fingers, the sensation, my weight on her hips, pushing her legs open.

"Good," I say. "That's good. You deserve a reward." I barely touch one finger between her lips, dip it in just a little, and wait for her to push against me, taking it inside. She does, immediately. Hard against me, pulling my index finger into her, the pulse of her around me, wet, slick and tight.

"This is beautiful," she whispers, closing her eyes.

"I want more than one finger inside you," I whisper. One of the few moments of explicit permission I'm going to pull from her.

She breathes out. "Yes, please." I love feeling as the muscles change and clench from inside. I leave my fingers still, let her move on them, two fingers, three. Moving inside, curling against the muscles, but not moving in and out.

She whispers yes. Yes. Her hips thrust against me. I can feel her, swollen, squeeze around my fingers, I raise myself above her, hold myself up; she knows why and unzips me, pulls out my cock; apparently this morning I had packed it just for her, yellow and solid and thick. She puts her fingers around it, feeling the length and girth of it. This wasn't planned. She's so open already, so expertly sliding her fingers along the shaft and head of it, pulling, tugging my hips toward her. I try not to think of what it would feel like sliding into her. It makes me wet and hard and sends my hips bucking without even trying.

Her mouth is open, legs open, arms reaching, eyes glazing and thick. "Please," she says, fast, whispering, just a hint of desperation behind her tongue. "I need it inside me."

I touch just the tip of it to her cunt and feel her pull

me inside. Then I am still again, I let my weight rest on top of her, just feeling her around me. I slowly pull out, then press back inside, deeper. She feels amazing under me like that. She's made for my cock, the exact contours of her were built for this moment, this motion, this cock inside of her, fitting perfectly.

"Take me, yes, I want you to take me," she whispers, gasping. "Yes … oh yes, exactly. Like that." She is so wet for me. Under me. She slides her fingers in my mouth and I suck. She touches her clit and I can feel her shudder while I'm inside and holding her.

"Let me come around you," she whispers into my neck, arms wrapped around my shoulders. I groan. God. I kiss her neck, her cheeks, her lips, her collarbone; press in and out of her, match her rhythm. I stay slow and soft and deep, over and over; look into her eyes, kiss her.

"God, you're so beautiful," I say.

"I'm so close," she gasps, eyes tightly shut, fingers digging into my arms, then looking up at me, right into my gasping face, panting, thrusting against me. "Do you want me come now, like this?"

She's under me, my cock in her, my weight on her, taking me in all the way, I can feel how tight her muscles are, pulling me in deep. I shudder, my eyes rolling. Fuck. Do I want her to come like this? Is there anything else I have ever wanted more? She could probably say anything and it would send me over the edge right now, but damn that was a good choice of words. The fucking nerve of her sometimes.

"Yes, god yes, I want you to come, just like this." Her legs are squeezing around me, her slick pussy lips around my cock, and she's kissing me until she can't and her mouth opens in a quiet scream, pushing against her muscles, against her body, against the edges. I feel her stomach curl and pulse. Her muscles tense, she gasps for air, the smallest smile on her lips. I keep my mouth on hers, hold her close to me, the weight of me on her, between her hips, still thrusting in her, steady and hard, until she shudders against me and makes me stop.

I hold her after, curl around her; feel her skin where her scars are, where she's bruised, where she's ticklish. But I have to go. I'm going to be behind already, will have to rush the rest of the afternoon. I pick up the thin white robe and slip it over her skin, then button my shirt, buckle my belt, tuck my shirt back in.

She walks me toward the door, hands me my clipboard with the florist orders on it, her signature bouncy in the middle of the top sheet. "So," I say, "who really sent the flowers?"

She shrugs, dismisses the question. "I wouldn't know."

"Come on, admit it. You sent them yourself. You knew I'd show up to deliver them."

"Are you kidding?" she asks. "As though I have time to hunt down every hot dyke I've crushed on." But she wouldn't have had to hunt me down. I've worked at this same place for years.

Rachel kisses me once more, and closes the door behind me. I believe her, almost.

Her Mouth on My Cock

That's all I really wanted, all night long, in those moments when we touched fingertips and knees sitting next to each other, the one time when I took her slender body into the circle of my arms and wrapped around her, cock tight against her and she could feel it, surely she could, moved her thigh against me and pulled her face away from nuzzling the nape of my neck to give me those eyes, those eyes, those pretty eyes, and my hand at the back of her neck where her hair is short and thin, delicate, dancing when she shakes her head or laughs which of course she does all night, mouth wide and open, lips pulled over teeth and oh I want to remember what that feels like, a girl on her knees, this girl, this girl on her knees in front of me with that tongue, that suckling throat of hers and she is so good at it, she has turned cock sucking into an art and somehow mine seems that much more real when a girl like this, a girl like her, who treats it as real, she doesn't care it is silicone, doesn't care I can't really feel it, not really, because she knows how I can feel it in my mind, knows that I know how it feels behind her teeth and it's Deep Throat as if her g-spot is at the roof of her mouth, as if she can actually orgasm from my cock, my blue plastic cock, in just the right spot and she's moaning, god, she's moaning and her vocal chords vibrate and I can feel it all the way through to my clit and the slick lips of my own cunt, buried, burrowed for a moment underneath this, this way my sex becomes outside my body, this way I become exposed and vulnerable and tender, revealing something of me, unpacking it all, taking it outside and asking to be seen, to be looked at, asking her to acknowledge my inability to do this for myself, to really have this body, to have this real cock, I am without, am not enough on my own, but I want to be this so badly I can create it in my mind, I can create it on my body, I can move within genders and beyond my own birth-assigned limitations to explore whatever it is I want to feel, and right now I want to feel my cock down her throat, I want to come in her mouth and feel her suck me dry, feel her suck the juice from me, shoot into her open throat and she takes me deeper, all the way to the base and her hands on my hips and ass to steady us both and I can barely stand up, my knees are buckling, hips bucking, she's looking up at me with those eyes again, those eyes, those pretty eyes, and I can hear her plead *let go, let go* like I've heard her say before, and she's so good at this, so fucking good, that I do, I do, I thrust against her, inside her, within her, and I am shriveled, rendered useless, spent.

I whimper; whisper, *Madeline, Madeline, Madeline,* again and again, and she wraps her arms around me, says *shhh* into the nape of my neck, and holds me close.

The Photo Shoot

She wants me.

Or, more accurately, I want her, and she's just starting to notice and respond. To begin to play in her mind with the idea of kissing me. She licks her lips without noticing, watching mine. Tucks her hair behind her ear. Gently blows her bangs out of her eyes.

I'm pinned behind the lens of her camera, which both magnifies me and puts a barrier between us.

But now she keeps letting the camera fall, looking at me bare.

"Shannon," I whisper. She's painting the lines of my masculinity with her photographer's eye. She has her elbow on her hip, camera cocked to the side. She snaps a few at this odd angle as her eyes wander.

The romantic love poem I was reciting by heart—to impress her, and to capture on film—is over. "Shannon," I say again, moving a step closer to her, out from the grey backdrop, the hooded lights. "Put the camera down."

Her eyes snap to attention, locked on my face. She moves slow and sets the camera on the nearby chair.

I curl her into my arms in one fluid motion, pull her to

me, her back perfectly nestled into my elbow. She breathes in sharply, the weight of her body leaning into me. She brings her hand to my chest, my collarbone, and lowers her eyes, looking at my mouth, my jaw, the stubble on my chin.

She's waiting. I trail my hand up her back, under her hair, and rest it on her neck. I place my other hand on her hip and push her away from me, bring her to me with the other, hovering her lips next to mine. She breathes in, her lips part, eyes close. I can smell her skin, her hair, her mouth, and I want to taste her.

I watch her struggle to release and resist the urge to lunge, press herself against me. She's moving toward me with tiny non-movements—her wrist, her thigh—and each time I am amused, aroused.

I am waiting for something.

Shannon doesn't sense that, and then she does, and her eyes open. She sees me watching her and I grin a little wider. I feel my cheeks pulled and those dimples appear. She makes that little gasp noise in her throat and lets her body go, her head drops, hips press into my hand and she lets me take the weight of her, and that's it, that's what it was, so I catch her as she gives in and I lunge.

We kiss. I don't start slow, but rather cover the full circle of her mouth with mine and pull her to me. She gives in, again. And oh, it is so beautiful.

Our kisses build and become longer, more insistent, more full of gasps. I have the pulse of her throat between my teeth, she pushes my suit coat from my shoulders, whispering, "God oh god oh god." Her murmur is prayer-like.

"Ohh you're going to fuck me aren't you?" she says, one leg slung up around my hip, skirt riding up. "Please tell me you're going to, please ..."

"Yeah," I say and take her lips back into my mouth.

"I'm going to fuck you."

I pull her other leg around my hip, lifting her off the ground and walking to the wall of windows, then place her into the window well, a convenient height from the floor. She catches my eye, looks momentarily shy, and lays back, spreading her legs.

Thigh-high stockings, soft skirt to her knees now pushed up to her hips. Her ankles and calves are delicately curved by her low heeled sandals. I pull her cream-colored, thin panties past her ankles and take her thighs in my hands, the soft soft skin of her, fingertips to her body teasingly slow, pressed against her, mouth to her nipples through her thin white blouse and bra, leaving a damp spot when I moved to her throat.

"God, oh god," she whispers on the exhale, slow and steady. She feels everything, every move of my teeth and lips, fingertips and hips, she responds so subtly and our bodies are dancing together like a waltz, like a tango, back and forth in the rhythm of our blood pressure pumping, our breath synched.

Her thighs are pressed back and she's pulling me in with magnetism, a force like gravity and my fingers are on her, swollen and sweet and slick. She's guiding me with subtle circles of her hips and I follow, I hear what she's asking through her body: *Touch here, no here. Deeper. Harder against my outer lips. Run your fingers up and down. Skate around my clit, dip your fingers in just a bit, just a little bit so I can feel stretched, two then three, then back to my clit and oh yes, right there, right there ...*

She tells me everything. I watch her mouth, her eyes, her skin flushed with heat.

"Oh yeah oh yeah, oh god yeah."

She's so gorgeous like this, all splayed open, head and neck pressed against the glass pane and knees to the deep walls of the window well. Hands pulling on my wrist, pushing on my chest, looped around my neck—*yes, there, oh right there*—and I feel her tightening and releasing from somewhere deep and I ache to be inside while she shudders, while she squeezes hard and ripples, beginning at the floor core of her, radiating up and out.

She looks at me when her body has calmed. Stares into me in a new way, eyes clear and shining. She swallows something that has dislodged and made its way to her tongue—a raw spark of energy and self and desire.

We slide to the floor; I shake out my forearm.

She's quiet, feeling exposed, and pulls her skirt back down. We curl around each other, holding, touching softly, my fingers on her shoulder, in her hair, now a mess of dirty blonde around her head. We lay breathing for a bit, then I start asking about her photography.

"Did you get the shot you wanted?" I ask. She rises to her elbows and looks at me again, as if remembering I am her subject.

"Mmm," she barely answers, tucking her hair behind her ear and then finding the top button of my Oxford with her slender fingers and pushing it through it's hole.

I watch. Oh, really. Raise my eyebrows. She says, "Well, I would like to see you in a few more ... positions." She giggles, I laugh. I lay back and let her pull my suspenders, peel my button-down, from my shoulders. She tosses it behind her and rises to her knees, taking off her buttoned blouse, knees apart, skirt loose, in her bra. She regards me with her photographer's eye again, puts her hands up in L shapes to frame the shot.

I grin, sheepish. Shannon reaches for my slacks; I knock her hand away. "Hey!" I feign protest. "What am I, a piece of meat?" She laughs, grabs at me again, unbuckles my belt, unzips my fly. I swat her hand again and she gives me a look, that look, that femme no-nonsense don't-fuck-with-me look that makes my cock throb.

I like power. I like that she has some. I can begin to taste what it'll be like to take it away.

I let her pull out my cock. I twist to reach my jacket, a crumpled heap on the floor, and pull a condom from the inner pocket. She watches me and her lips part, mouth waters—I can see it.

She laughs, tossing her hair, eyes alight. "Is that what you think?" she says, playful, but it's a sensitive enough old wound that I freeze for a second. *Wait, what? Isn't that—didn't she want—weren't we going to—*

She laughs again at my flustered face, then crawls toward me, straddling my legs as I sit on the floor, leaning back on my hands. She pushes against my chest until I'm lying all the way against the floor.

"You're going to have to try a little harder than that," she teases, laying her body on top of mine, our mouths close. I grin, shift my shoulders, wrap my arms around her naked waist as she keeps her hands by my ears, holding herself up. With a swift, sudden motion I flip her onto her back and roll on top of her, carefully switching my hips so my exposed cock is between her legs. I leave my hands on the curve of her hips and begin to feel hungry for her again, palmfuls of skin, stomach exposed, breasts moving gently with her inhales and exhales which are increasing as she lifts her hips up into me, which gets me hard.

I groan a little into her neck, teeth to her collarbone, her shoulders. She begins struggling, pushes against me with her arms, attempts to flip me with her legs. I almost let her think she can as she moves the weight of me around; I'm testing her strength. I swiftly stop her by taking both of her wrists in my hands, pressing them into the floor, grinding my hips against hers.

She stops struggling. I feel the grin on my mouth again.

I like how she brings the cockiness out of me.

She smirks at my victory smile. "Well, you are at a distinct advantage, being on top."

"You were on top a minute ago."

"Yeah, but … uh …"

"Mmm hmmm." I shift above her head and hold both of hers with one of mine, bite her chest, the tops of her exposed breasts where my mouth can reach under her bra. She inhales, arching her back and attempting to free her wrists from my grip.

"What am I going to do with you," I mutter into her skin, my mouth on that spot between her breasts, on her smooth stomach, as far down as I can go without losing the grip on her hands. I press harder against her subtle struggling.

"Oh, oh god," she starts again as I manage to take one of her nipples into my mouth. I let my other hand travel the length of her body, between her legs, and find that she eagerly opens, and she's wet.

I get distracted, a growl of want lodged in my throat, and she suddenly manages to slip out of my grip and scurries out from under me. I grab for her leg, then ankle, as I see her nearly escape my reach, and she attempts to shake me off, laughing. I scramble after her, grabbing at whatever I can, her knee, her shoes, and get hold of the fabric of her skirt which, she wriggles out of and off. I catch her thigh with my fingers and squeeze, hard.

She gasps—"Dammit, that's gonna bruise!"—and steals a playful glance back at me. I grab for her hips, nearly wishing I had nails so she would feel me dig into her, my grip as a barb she was clearly rubbing the wrong way.

"Where the hell do you think you're going," I grumble, low and strong, which stops her. My grip on her body pulls both me to her and her to me and we match suddenly, my slacks between her legs, stockings below her knees, thighs bare and exposed. I lower my face to hers and take one more fist of hair, pressing her shoulder into the wood floor, pressing my knees up under her thighs which forces hers apart. I watch her face for just a moment as she's pinned under me, and let her feel it.

I lift myself to my knees and rescue the condom from the floor nearby, tearing it open with my teeth. The plastic gives way easily, and I roll it over my cock, holding it in my hand for a moment, enjoying the feel of the girth, the weight of it in my palm.

She's only breathing, watching me. My mouth waters and I spit into my palm, rub the length of the shaft. Inadequate lube, but it's something. She's bending her knees together and looking bashful, feeling exposed again, but her face is full of lust. Her body writhes a little and she tries to keep still.

I stay kneeling and pull her to me, her thighs over mine so I'm under her hips and her ass is just a little off the floor. I tease her cunt with my fingers, lightly, soft, and watch her face. I've already done this once, I have a better idea of how she likes it. Slow, with pressure. Harder here when she presses into my hand. Skating around her lips soft and supple. I slide two fingers inside easily, then three, watching her face as she gasps and smiles, working my fingers in her harder, a little quicker. Her cunt thickens, sweet, and she lets me in.

I slide her swiftly onto my cock, switch my hands to her hips, pulling her against me, thrusting.

"Fuck, oh fuck ..."

So beautiful, split open by my cock. Stretching her legs wide to take me deeper. She's so good.

She brings her palms to the floor above her head to keep from sliding and presses into me deeper, mouth open, hair wild and in her eyes. I increase my pace and she follows me, lets me lead her, and we both build until we're groaning, yelling out, muscles straining in rhythm, my head bent back, back arched.

"Oh god oh god, oh fuck," she gasps. "Fuck, fuck!" I'm nearly shouting out too, right along with her, grunts of working my body, hands slipping on her hips from sweat.

I collapse suddenly, pushed to a small peak of a limit, over her, and she pushes me and rolls me onto my back, straddling and sitting on top of me, knees by my thighs. I keep my legs close together and she rocks her hips back and forth, writhing, as I take hold of her shoes, get a grip on the heels and pull her to me. She slides two fingers into her mouth and wets her fingertips, then reaches her hand to her clit and starts moving in small circles, closing her eyes and bending her head back. She brings her other hand to her head and pushes her hair out of her eyes, attempts to tuck it behind her ear but it falls right away, rocking harder, squeezing my cock harder, circling harder, and my hips are bucking fast, meeting hers.

"Oh god oh god, god oh god," she mutters, a long, soft string of words, hips strong and hard against mine. I let go of her heels and move my hands to her hips again which gives me a better grip on our rhythm, and I take control of the pace, fuck her hard from underneath her, fucking up into her deep and she starts screaming, I feel her entire body contract around me and her back arches, mouth opens, head falls back until her body shudders, stomach contracts hard and she shakes, shoulders bowing, falling forward onto my chest as shockwaves roll through her.

I run my fingers through her hair, down her back, over the contours of her hips for a minute. "Fuck," I whisper into her hair, "that was so damn hot."

Her breathing has slowed and she lifts her head to look

at me, bashful, aware of herself again. She smiles and kisses me, full of tongue and desire and release, skin flushed and beautiful, just beautiful.

"Where's your camera?" I say. "I want to capture you just like this."

Bully

She is face-down, ponytail bobbing, wrists and ankles tied to my bedposts, the simple steel I won from my last breakup. Since then, I have fucked five women in this bed. She is the sixth.

Does it matter how I got her here? Whether I wined and dined her, bought her indulgent fruity mixed drinks, a delectable dinner, her body now satiated but wanting other fullness, wanting me to stop fingering my fork spoon knife glass napkin ice cubes and begin placing my hands carefully on her skin.

Or perhaps I simply ordered her over here, sent a car to her apartment and was waiting downstairs when she arrived at mine, paid the driver, removed my dark tie from the tight collar of my baby-blue button down and slipped it over her eyes. Lead her up two flights of stairs without her sense of sight.

No matter. She's been here before. Nothing to see.

I am tempted to rip seams, pop buttons open with force. She knows how she brings that out in me.

Instead, I make her wait. Drag the thin fabric of her shirt along her skin, slow as I can. She can't see, but she can feel me, my breath on her, my hands, my rough thumbs waiting to dig bruises into her upper arms, stomach, hips.

My collection of floggers hang from a swirl of Victorian iron on the wall next to my bed. I choose my favorite: black, thin leather, red deerskin flanks in the center.

She's stripped, naked except for the dark blue schoolboy tie around her eyes. I know it's not foolproof, other blindfolds are more efficient. I don't mind the glimpses she steals.

She see me strip down to loose, soft cotton jersey boxers and an a-shirt. Have to have my arms free if I'm going to beat her, after all. My cock pokes through the single button in the boxers. She likes it when it does that.

I smell like summer and sweat, and I've been drinking bourbon again, on the rocks, just a little. She smells sweet. Fresh. Clean like linen. My mouth waters and I imagine my tongue tracing the curves of her lower back, up to her shoulder, the back of her neck.

I stand gazing for too long, and she begins to squirm.

"Be still," I say, and put one hand on her ass, trace it down to the back of her knee. "I'm going to hit you now."

She lets out a puff of air that is a whimper and a sigh. Her skin tenses and she tries to counter by keeping her muscles calm.

"Relax," I say, "or it'll just hurt more."

I want her to count to fifty, but wonder if that's too many. I like flogging with an end in sight. Otherwise I go into that physiological trance state where I find rhythm and forget to stop.

I begin counting in my head. One—thump. Two—thump. Her muscles begin to open but still wince just before the leather makes contact.

Five—thump.

Six—thump.

The leather makes a small whoosh through the air. I'm

being gentle, mostly just a tap, letting gravity pull the tassels to her skin, her ass, her thighs.

Whoosh—ten—thump.

Whoosh—eleven—thump.

I begin to throw a little more arm strength into the flogger and she grunts with an *uh*, wincing a little stronger.

At fifteen I pause, run my hand, fingers, palm, along her skin. Tender where I've hit her hardest. She inhales sharply and arches her back to the touch, like a cat.

"Your skin looks beautiful," I say. "It's beginning to pinken, a little, at the edges." My mouth is at her neck and I kiss her a few times, find her panting, tongue swollen.

"More, darling?" I ask, an offer and a question. She turns her face toward the sound of my voice, bites her lower lip, and nods.

"Oh—yes—please—" she manages.

She does beg real pretty. I'll never forget her legs wrapped around me that night I refused to slide inside her until she begged.

She'd said, finally: "Oh baby, your cock is so sweet, so sweet and hard, fill me up with it, baby, shove it in me, please, pump it in me, let me milk it, let me squeeze it hard till you come inside me, oh please I want it—I need it—I wanna be filled up—please put it in, please."

It was the way her eyes flashed on that last *please* that did it to me. Finally sent me over desire's edge to where I had to take her.

Tonight, I'm ready to hold out.

I switch up my rhythm so the flogger first hits my back over my right shoulder, then her back and exposed ass, then I catch it with my left hand. Easier on a Saint Andrew's Cross than lying down, but I like the way it stings my palm. Plus I can gauge the strength of the blows this way.

Shoulder—ass—hand. Twenty.

Shoulder—back—hand. Twenty one.

Shoulder—ass—hand. Twenty two.

She's writhing a bit, whimpering at the blows, occasional head back open-throated gasp when I land somewhere particularly hard.

Shoulder—back—hand. Twenty five.

I decide to go to thirty. Her skin is reddened to how I like it, ripe, her hips are making these nice s-curves and I want to fuck her ass.

I increase not just the muscle power I'm putting behind the flogger but also the velocity. Harder. Faster. She cries out. Twenty seven. She gasps and cries out again. Twenty eight.

I grab her hair, a neat twist in a ponytail, and lift her head slightly, my mouth by her ear. I drag the flogger along her inner thighs.

"Quiet," I mutter.

She sighs and shudders. "You're such a bully," she whispers, taunting, not exactly intending for me to hear her.

I want to growl, but instead I push her cheek to the soft sheet and hold her there by the back of her neck, aiming a few blows between her legs.

Leather on labia. My favorite.

She's whimpering again. I lose count and take five or six quick whaps to her cunt and inner thighs. She is making noises that sound like exquisite agony.

I step out of my boxers (they're in the way), lube up my cock from the pump on the bedside table and moisten two fingers, then kneel between her thighs and lube her asshole, fingering the crack of her ass. I slide the thumb of my left hand into her slick wet cunt and can feel her clit under my index finger, so I set it there and rock it gently back and forth. The heel of my hand spreads her labia and tilts her pelvis back and up. It serves her to me like a feast.

She moans. The blindfold has slipped over her head and she's watching me from over her left shoulder.

I slide one finger, then two, into her tight asshole while leaving my other hand still, fingers inside her. She groans a little and presses into me harder. I slide my fingers out and touch the tip of my dick to her tight hole and she swallows it, opens to it, and I can feel the muscles stretch and pulse when the head of my cock pops in, the shaft of it sliding easier through the tightest places.

She is still moaning. Sounds from her mouth as she grinds back into me and wiggles her hips against mine. She's almost on her knees and elbows now, hands gripped around the ties that hold her to the headboard. Lower back arched, still a little pink.

I let go of the cupped grip on her cunt and find her hipbones with my palms, pushing her from me and pulling her back so I don't have to clench, I just move her. I pull her ass down onto my cock, feeling the resistance in her tight hole. It's so good fucking her this way. My thighs and ass are clenched, clit rubbing against the base of my cock every time I thrust inside. Easing forward so my thighs hit hers. Working in and out faster, a little, harder, my body an S-curve from knee to stomach, not just in-out but rolling against her. She is open-mouth screaming into the pillow and asking for more, *harder, oh god, fuck me, fuck my ass* and I slap against her, once, twice, both of us groaning.

My head rolls back, my back curves, pounding against her harder as my orgasm comes closer, the resistance of her ass offering me tight pressure every time I thrust inside. My hands still hold her hips, her ass, the sit-bones of her ass as my cunt pulses, cock fucks.

She can feel it in me. "Do it," she says, "come in my ass, fuck me till you come, do it harder, thrust inside me—" And I groan, yelling *oh god oh god yes, fuck,* and shudder against her until I'm spent, throw my arm around her waist and collapse on top of her, kissing her neck, her shoulders.

I breathe heavy as my body and her body calm, then finally I slip out and untie her. She curls next to me, knees and arms between us as we both lay on our sides and I gently finger her wrists, ankles, the places you were bound, and her back, shoulders, ass. Places I hit you. Tender.

"Alright?" I ask. We gaze at each other.

She smiles. "Course." She holds my cheek in her palm and I kiss her thumb. "You?"

"Mmmm," I manage, grinning. Spent. She didn't come, this time. "I'll make it up to you in the morning," I promise, grateful she's let me take what I've been craving. I'll give her whatever she wants.

She runs her fingers through my short boy hair. "Damn right you will," she says, and pulls the covers up over us both.

Finding a Third

Brett reaches up with one hand and peels off my purple tie, her blindfold, sticky against her forehead. Her mouth is full of her girlfriend's cock. I watch her hesitate momentarily until she wiggles her hips a little, which is my acknowledgement. If her girlfriend is in her mouth, I must be the one fucking her from behind.

I hadn't expected the evening to go this way. I had hoped to take Brett back to my place, sure, but as soon as her handsome and clearly doting soft butch girlfriend showed up while I was easily fingering Brett's jean-clad knee, I altered my evening expectations.

"Oh, you're ... spoken for," I say, pouting, exaggerating my disappointment in order to hide it. "Too bad. Unless ... I don't suppose you'd want to share?" I look to the girlfriend. Eli. She sizes me up, then looks at Brett. Brett's eyes sparkle and she cracks into a cheeky half-smile. I think Eli is about to punch me, and they'd have a fun night of what-if sex, then I think Brett might ditch Eli by the way she's already started to devouring me with those smoldering looks, then I think Eli left Brett alone for just this reason: to find a third. I consider making a joke to Brett about feeling used, how I'd been on my very best charming pick-up-the-hottest-girl-at-the-bar behavior, but decide against it.

"Yeah, alright." Eli shifts her weight, digs her hands into her pockets, also with a slight half-smile. She has nice arms: strong, defined muscles under her white tee shirt. She's more androgynous than I am, but still more boyish than Brett, who calls herself a subtle femme. "May take a second glance, but it's there," she told me.

That subtle femme caught my eye as soon as she walked in the bar. Nice ass, graceful legs. Pretty eyes behind her thick, long curly hair. Cute glasses that enhance the curves of her jaw and cheeks.

I drain what's left of my melted ice and Jameson. Their hotel is on the corner.

I untie my purple silk tie in the elevator. "Kiss her," I say to Eli. She's not sure she wants to take orders from me, but she wants to kiss Brett and she's glad I didn't move in to kiss her myself. Brett is curled against the corner of the elevator, watching us both interacting. She sometimes raises a finger to her mouth as if to bite her nail.

Eli carefully places each hand on the elevator wall behind Brett and leans in to kiss her. Brett watches me, still unslipping my tie, carefully undoing the knots, mouth moving against Eli, eyes open. I undo the top button of my black button-down shirt and hold one side of the tie in each hand.

And so it begins.

The elevator doors open, I step through and wait for them to lead the way. A cute couple, attractive. Brett has a great ass.

Eli slides her keycard in and the trio of us enters the bland hotel room. Two beds, small table with an ice bucket and glasses, a chair that is a cheap knock-off of something comfortable. Their suitcases are on one bed. The other is perfectly made.

I toss the tie to Eli. "Care to blindfold her?" Brett turns to me, eyes wide, still quiet. Eli smiles and tosses it back to me. "You do it," she says, crossing her arms over her chest. She's smiling but also challenging me. I don't understand this game yet.

I take two steps to Brett, who has sought protection from a wall again. I take her glasses and set them on the bed with the open suitcases. Her hair falls in her face, chin tipped down. Curls everywhere. I want handfuls of it. Fistfuls and to use it as rope, as something by which to pull her. It is long, past her shoulders. It would splay out everywhere. I finger her jaw, her cheekbone.

We have a moment. Eye contact, connecting. "Can I kiss you?" I ask. I'm asking her if she's okay with this. She's stealing sipping glances at me, looking down at my hands on her waist, looking back up, body language telling me she loves it, is just a little shy, but she likes to be told what to do.

She nods. Murmurs something that sounded like *please* or *yes*, or maybe it is just *mmm*. Her body goes soft against me and her hands find my waist, then lower back, then fingers dig into my shoulders as I kiss her. I like the way Brett lets go, trusts, lets me push her by my energy and intention. She picks up on the subtleties fast.

I draw her thin tee shirt over her head, a mess of dark curls spilling out. Eli is at her back now, unhooking her bra, hands on her skin, her stomach, her shoulders, kissing her neck, rolling her nipples between her fingers and Brett leans back into her, one arm up, hand in Eli's short cropped hair.

I slide my wide purple tie over Brett's eyes and tie it behind her head.

Eli has her strap-on in one fist and the vinyl harness dangles from her hand.

"You may not be able to tell who is doing what," Eli

says, still at Brett's neck, watching me as I unbutton the rest of my shirt, slipping it off of my shoulders. "But I'll be here the whole time," she promises, still holding Brett close. I'm already strapped, she needs a minute to prep. I take Eli's hand from Brett's shoulder and we both step back, stand and watch Brett reaching for us by listening to where we are moving. I keep Eli's hand a moment and kiss her fingers, suck her first finger onto my tongue, flick it with my tongue piercing.

"Butch on butch," she says, laughing, her eyes soft. "That's practically faggotry."

"Best kind of faggotry, in my opinion," I say, and lightly whap the ass of her jeans as I step back to Brett.

"Tell her to get on her knees," I say to Eli.

"Get on your knees," Eli says, unbuttoning and sliding her jeans off, pulling the harness on.

Brett sinks. She brings her hands behind her back and I put my hands in her hair, then move one to my fly and cock. I finger her lips, pretty mouth, and she takes two of my fingers between her teeth, sucks them onto her tongue. Soft.

Actions become blurred. My cock. Brett jeans tossed on the floor. Eli fingering Brett while Brett sucks me, the lovely noises from her throat as she tries not to come, not yet. Eli clearly knows what to do and doesn't let up, Brett arches her back like a cat and nearly hangs from my legs, gripping my thighs with her hands as she sucks my cock, pulling on my jeans until they come down with my briefs and she slides two fingers under my favorite harness to find my clit. She works it soft and quick, strokes it and rolls it gently between her fingers. I groan, hips bucking. Lord.

Eli has one hand on her left hip, still working her right hand between Brett's legs.

Brett starts shuddering and panting and she's going to come, I don't know if I should pull out of her mouth or stay.

She stops sucking but keeps leaning forward into my cock, breathing heavy around it, big gasps of air mouth open and I let her work herself against it, and she does, god she does, until she's writhing and rocking against me, my hips and cock, against Eli and her hands, shuddering, convulsing at the stomach in small pulses of muscle and breath and she groans, hard, gasps for air, whimpers a little, and is still.

Eli holds her hips for a minute, letting her rest in her crumpled state on the beige hotel carpet, then twirls her finger at me, meaning time to switch.

My mouth waters.

Eli still doesn't have her cock on. Her harness is loose but won't fall off her hips; she's stripped her white tee shirt and jeans. I remove my jeans and watch as Eli guides Brett from the floor onto the bed, onto her back, Brett's knees hanging off the end, legs parted but together, thighs pressing.

Kneeling on the bed, Eli slowly draws one knee to either side of Brett's shoulders, then lowers her cunt gently down over Brett's mouth. I realize my jeans are stuck at my ankles and try to tear my eyes away long enough to pull them all the way off.

Eli has hold of the wall-mounted headboard and her head is thrown back a little, spine already arching, body moving eagerly. Brett's knees are bent, running one foot over the other, up her calf. She has hold of Eli's thigh and her body is curling off the bed like she is about to levitate.

I leave my a-shirt on and move to the foot of the bed, touch Brett's knees, caress her thighs, her calves as much as I can reach, her hipbones, the gentle hair over her pussy, her labia, swollen and sensitive. I ease her left knee off the bed into the grip of my elbow and step closer, use my right knee to press her legs open. She's slick, wet and supple, muscles pliable, she lets me move her where I want her. Her hands reach for me a second then back to Eli's lower back and thighs. Eli is quietly moaning.

I feel her cunt with two fingers and slide in slow to get the angle, feel how deep she is. My packing cock isn't huge but it is enough. She is slick and smooth and she parts her thighs a little farther, offering herself a little more.

I let my fingers wander over her labia and clit as the head of my dick finds her opening and slides in. A little too fast and she gasps. Her whole body responds, she groans, a sound that starts deep in her belly, somewhere my cock is hitting. Her sounds are muffled vibrations against Eli's cunt.

Eli is working harder against Brett, increasingly faster, pressing her hips down into Brett's face, balancing herself against the headboard and wall. She is practically on all fours, kneeling, working her clit in Brett's mouth.

I match Eli's rhythm and pace and speed. Slow strokes in and out, then faster, shallow. Sometimes a little rotation, a side-to-side motion. I copy her precisely.

They are both moaning. I tighten my grip on Brett's hips and find a sweet spot, start thrusting harder. I hear Eli's orgasm building, she's gasping now and moaning in longer drawn-out sounds. Eli's whole body begins to shiver and I barely notice, I am occupied, Brett has her legs wrapped around my waist and she's pulling me in, hard and deep.

Eli swings one leg over and half slides off the bed. Her legs are a little weak.

"Turn," Eli says, pushing at Brett from the side. Brett turns to her stomach. Eli grabs her cock from the foot of the other bed as I don't wait, but slide right back in, tip to balls, and begin fucking Brett again like I never stopped. She has one knee on the bed, one leg over the edge, toes on the floor, pelvis tilted up and back to take me in. Her hands are grabbing fistfuls of blankets and peeling the sheets from the bed. Her hair falls in a mess of curls around her head, only slightly restrained by my purple tie still around her forehead.

My head leans back, shoulders back, holding onto Brett's hips, sometimes the flesh of her ass, round and a nice handful. Eli slides back onto the bed, sits with her back against the headboard and pulls Brett to her, sliding her cock into Brett's mouth.

I'm close to coming and feel pressure building, the muscles contracting with new force and urgency, when Brett lifts her hand off the bed and removes the blindfold. I see Eli smile at her, hands in her hair, then look at me. We lock eyes for just a moment, until Brett presses her hips back and wiggles against me, and the sensation is overwhelming, throwing me off balance and sounds escape my throat with every exhale until I'm pounding, pumping hard against her and Brett is gasping into Eli's cock, muffled, and it all builds, hard, until I swear I can feel her cunt contracting around my cock, squeezing, and I explode inside her, coming hard, rocking against her, shaking.

My lower back is wet with sweat and I stagger a little, knees weak, joints not holding me up, and both Brett and Eli are looking at me, biting back grins, giggling, ecstatic. I swallow embarrassment and clear my throat, which makes them laugh more. I laugh too. We're all a bit high. I lay myself down next to Brett, awkwardly, not able to quite be all the way on the bed but the support feels good, and I'm breathing hard, still catching my breath.

Eli laces her fingers through Brett's and kisses her. "That was fun," she says between kisses. "Sharing you. So... when is it not rude to kick them out?"

I laugh, kiss Brett with my hand in her hair, kiss Eli gently on the lips, cupping her chin, then pull on my jeans. I can take a hint.

The Straight Girl at the Dyke Bar

I'm out back, in the alley behind the dive dyke bar, when she finds me. She busts through the door with a fruity indulgent mixed drink in her hand and I fear for her balance.

"There you are," she says. "I thought I saw you come this way."

I'm puzzled. I don't know who she is. "Are you okay?"

Her eyes flash and she lets the back door close on its hinge with a bang. "Yes," she said, like it was obvious. "Clearly."

I take one last drag of my American Spirit and flick the butt into the dumpster. "What are you doing?"

"Isn't it obvious?" she slurrs, just a little. "I'm trying to seduce you." She is right next to me, my height, but she keeps her eyes low and looks up at me with submission. My internal butch cock stirs.

"You're drunk," I say.

"Yeah." She steps closer and bites at her lips, looking at mine.

"Are you here with friends? Maybe they should take you home."

"I don't think so. I'm not ready to go home."

"You're drunk," I say again.

"Not so drunk that I don't know what I want," she snaps. "Only drunk enough that I can go after it." She inches closer to me. My mouth waters. I want my hands on the curves of her waist, her hips, her ribcage. I struggle to keep my cool.

"What are you doing ... here?" I almost say *in a gay bar*.

She sneers. "I know, I'm the only straight girl. I usually am. Well. Whatever." Her tone changes. "I know how this sex thing works," she purrs, palm of her hand against my zipper where my cock is hard, straining against my jeans. The pressure of her fingers feels exquisite.

I knock her hand away. "Hey."

She withdraws and slowly moves her fingers up my arm, feeling the muscles, tendons. Circles her fingers around my wrist. "Come on," she whispers. "I saw you watching me."

Her neck is dangerously close to my mouth and I can smell her, sweet and thick. I want a mouthful of her perfume. Teeth on her skin. My hands move—practically involuntarily—to the curves she lays out for me, the precise placement of her body next to mine inviting my touches.

She tilts her face toward mine. Half-closes her eyes. I don't even know her name. My friends are still inside, probably waiting for me. It is getting late. The alley is filthy. She smells so delicious. The desire between us is pooling and tangible.

Her body is small, my hands with fingers spread cover her back. I bring them up under her hair, pull her toward me, take ahold of the back of her skull and neck. She leans into me.

"Okay," I say, watching her face as our lips barely brush while I speak. "But we're going to do this my way."

I bring my lips down on hers hard, crushing, devouring, insistent. She whimpers, back curving. I hold her body at the precise angle and distance that I want, and she goes limp in my arms, giving over, arms and shoulders falling back, on her toes.

Pulling away, I grin. Take a step back. Keep my eyes on her, touch my lower lip with my thumb and feel that stirring in my stomach, that desire, that power. Her eyes get a little shimmery and she attempts to keep her tough look, but it is a mask I will un-peel.

I close the distance between us. Trace my fingers down her left arm until I reach her hand, still holding that delicate glass of fruity alcohol, and I take it from her. I make eye contact, and then quickly I toss it—hard, overhand, arm flexing—at the blank space where the building meets the concrete in the alley. It shatters brilliantly, a cascade of glass, the sound filling the narrow space between the buildings.

She watches my arm, the glass, the crash. We turn our eyes back to each other, hers open, mouth open, the small of her back arching. Her mouth waters and she moves her jaw, I can see it. Subtle. She wants to lunge for me. Good girl, she stays still.

Hardening my glance, I move toward her, thick, keeping distance between us, and she stumbles back, her low heels catching on the uneven pavement, thrusting her hands out behind her but I keep eye contact, keep two fingers on her waist and lead her back, back, until she is against the dumpster. She swallows. It is wider at the top than the bottom, slanting out; she cowers under it a little.

I lift my chin, once. "Hold that."

She does. Lifts her arms to grip the edge of the dumpster. Makes a face. "It feels gross."

"Mmm." *You're getting fucked in an alley behind a dive bar. What do you expect?* I thrust my hand between her legs. Her skirt is tight—I pull at it, shove it up her thighs to expose her, pull tight against the lacy fabric of her panties and press two fingers inside her. Smooth. She inhales, moans.

"So wet," I say, mouth against her cheek. She keeps ahold of the edge with her hands, arms raised. My body is perpendicular to hers, cock against her hip. I work my fingers inside, slick and slow and deep, thumb on her clit, on that spot below her clit, my hand gripping her pubic bone.

She moans, knees weakening, hips dipping down to take in more of me. I add a third finger. "You know how to get fucked, don't you."

Mouth gaping, she breathes heavily, turning her head and sucking on her lips. I can feel my fingers working a good spot inside her and she is increasingly sensitive, reactive to my pressing and curling, thumb flicking a little lighter and faster on her clit. Her thighs shake and she lifts one leg off the ground, bends her knee, presses her legs apart and against me, body shaking against me, until she gasps hard and I feel the ring of muscles inside her grip my fingers, hard, her clit fat and sensitive and pressing against my thumb, throbbing, until she shudders, bucks her hips, begins to lose her balance and leans against me, gasping, little moans coming from her throat.

She looks up at me, winds her arms around my neck. "I don't usually come so fast," she says, a little apologetically.

I shake my head and smile. "I'm not done with you yet." I don't wait, but take her wrists in my hands and put them back up onto the dumpster's edge, then twist her body so she faces away from me, pull her skirt up over her ass, and unzip my fly. She moans and arches her back, displays her pussy to me. I pull my cock out, and sheathe it quickly with a condom from my back pocket.

With one hand I push aside her panties, slightly stretched now anyway; and with the other I press her ass apart, then guide my cock into her wet hole. It stretches her as I pump in and out, smooth slow long strokes, my hips in circles, working the cock against my clit as much as inside her.

My release builds easily in me after the way she came and it doesn't take long for me to grip her hips like handles and begin pounding, shifting my feet to stabilize my movement, muscles in my thighs hard and contracted, groaning and grunting with the physical effort of it all. She presses hard with her hands against the disgusting dumpster, arching her back and pushing against me, receiving me as I fuck harder, pulling almost all the way out and then slickly entering her again, the length of my cock, pressing myself tight against her ass and hips in rocking little thrusts, until I find that sweet spot and my clit contracts and I see myself exploding in her, which makes me come harder, muscles thick and shuddering, gasping, until I slow my pace against her and come to stillness. I peel myself off her back.

She watches me over her shoulder, all eyes and hair, desire still in her face, painted over her cheeks, then rises and straightens her skirt, smooths her hair. I tuck my cock back into my briefs and zip my jeans.

She smiles at me, then starts giggling, then laughing hard, full-bodied from her stomach, eyes sparkling. I'm amused, and puzzled. "What's so funny?"

"So," she giggles, wrapping her arms around my neck and tossing her hair. "You're awfully cute. Come here often? Can I buy you a drink?"

I laugh, holding her in a full-body embrace before I separate and kiss her pretty mouth. "Sure. Why not." I step up the three low rickety back stairs and open the back door to the bar, letting her step in first. Jukebox tunes and pool cues and women's laughter spill out.

I see a few of my buddies at a table in the corner. They

watch me come back in with my hand on the back of the girl. They make faces and gestures and raise their eyebrows. I shush them with a look, turning my attention back to her.

"I, uh, I didn't get your name," I say, trying to remember my manners.

"That's because I didn't say," she answers, hips switching as she dodges through the crowd and steps up to the bar, immediately getting the bartender's attention. Glancing at me sideways, she says, "Jameson on the rocks, for Sinclair."

Popsicle in the Library

"You know there's no food allowed in the library," I growl in her ear, pressing her stomach against the concrete stairwell wall. I'm speaking quietly but it still echoes.

"Unh," she groans, her tongue not able to form words, mouth open.

"Not very polite of you, breaking the rules like that." I lift her dress and shove my hands under the edge of her panties. She's wet.

"Oh, you like this, do you? You're enjoying this?" I flick my fingers over her cunt, then pull my hand away. She whimpers, echoing in the stairwell.

"You want something to suck on, girl, you take this." I let up on the pressure against her. She peels her cheek away from the concrete. I take my hand from her hair and unzip my fly, pull out my packing cock and bend it straight. "Go on, suck it."

She drops to her knees, lips red from the cherry popsicle she'd been sucking lewdly when I walked up to her. I'd thought we'd had a study date. Her legs were all long in the windowsill, summery dress light and airy and when she moved her knees I could see the thin cream fabric covering her pussy, the outline of her lips, plump, thick.

She offered the sweet, bright red popsicle to me. "Want some?" Eyes all sly and sparkly, playful smile on her mouth.

I shook my head no. Crossed my arms over my chest. Raised one eyebrow and nodded for her to continue.

She did. Slid the whole thing into her mouth and sweet red cherry juice drips down her chin.

And now she sucks me just like she was working that sticky treat, sucking it like she could pull the juice from me too, like she could use the muscles in her cheeks to draw the cum from me and swallow it all.

Fuck. I want her to make me shoot in her mouth like that. Oh I wish I could.

I groan. "Enough," I say and pull her to her feet. I don't take her panties off, just lift her dress and finger the fleshy parts of her ass with my hand, then give it a good smack.

Not too hard. I cup my palm a little bit and it echoes perfectly, which makes the slight sting more impressive because it sounds so loud. I smack again. She cries out a little. Again, harder, and she yelps, I hear it floors away. My cock is still out and I shove it into her. Hard. Slide it in all the way. She whimpers, presses her hands into the concrete, the side of her face, presses her ass into me, spreads her legs.

She actually shouts, my thrusts pounding the noise out of her.

"Quiet," I say, harsh, in her ear.

She is still whimpering. Trying to be quiet and she whispers, "I'm gonna spew if you keep fucking me like that."

"Oh yeah? You're a messy one, eh? Bring it on. Come on, come for me." My mouth at her ear and my hands on her hips, head of my cock hitting her g-spot, I can feel it, and she comes hard, wet, dripping, soaking my cock, her thighs, the floor, my shoes. Her body shudders but that's not all I can get out of her and I pull out and twist her around before she's regained her composure, slide my fingers in, slide my hand in, reach up and inside her and I can feel the spots to press and I do.

I growl, "Do it again." She shakes her head *no* but she's gasping, legs wide and on her tiptoes on the wet floor. She grabs for my wrist to pull me back, embarrassment in her eyes and she can feel her own cum dripping down her legs, but I don't let up.

I take hold of her hair with my other hand and pull her head back, press my mouth to her jaw saying, "Come on, I'm gonna make you. You're going to come just for me. Fuck yeah, do it. I'm gonna make you, fuck yeah, fuck yeah."

And she wraps her arms around my neck and comes, and comes, and comes.

Her Best Line

I've heard the New York City subway referred to as a "hotbed of sin," and it's true: New York has the most attractive people wearing their most attractive fashion and looking for the most exciting encounter at every given moment.

Tonight, I'm on my way to meet the gang, play some pool, drink more whiskey, share hook-up stories, and talk about how we're all just sensitive, emotional butches underneath the tough exterior.

She gets on at 9th Street, I notice her immediately. Petite, dark hair, gold glowing skin, big dark eyes, a thin swingy white wrap dress tied at her hip, simple white sandals with a small kitten heel and four straps over her ankles. She sits across from me and doesn't notice me, she's absorbed in Murakami's *The Wind-Up Bird Chronicle*.

She's gorgeous. She crosses and uncrosses her legs slowly, deliberately. She's got this smoky eye makeup on that makes her dark brown eyes even bigger, liquid and pooling and I haven't seen her lower her lids and look up under her lashes, but I'd like to.

I wonder if she's queer. Then I wonder if that matters.

Sure it does—it's more fun to sleep with a girl who knows how to treat a butch in bed. We're strange creatures, to some, after all. I think what I often think when I see a gorgeous, leggy girl, reading some intellectual book, in barely enough clothing: if she's queer, man, all is right with the world. I keep an eye on her, watching her movements, the way she brings a fingertip to her mouth and laughs to herself, the way her eyes dart, how her palm flips as she turns pages. She leaves her legs uncrossed once and turns her ankle in slightly, an unconscious but slightly submissive move that makes my hands ache.

I turn up my iPod, attempting to stop staring. She slips me a tiny bit of eye contact, just a sip, and a sideways smile that says she's known I was there all along.

Damnit.

I shift unconsciously, take my leg down from the seat in front of me and cross my legs, sit up straight. My cock shifts wrong in that maneuver and now it is digging into my inner thigh, but I can't adjust it—how tacky to go poking at my junk when she's watching. I can't shift my position again yet either or she'll know I am adjusting myself for her gaze. I'm starting to wince from the way the cock is pressing into me, dull pain that may be making a bruise. That'll be attractive.

I try to look casual and stare out the window as the subway takes the Manhattan bridge into the city. She turns pages, crosses her legs again. I reach into my pocket and finger one of my cards with only my name and cell number, black text on a simple white background. Classic. Minimal. I don't need adornment. Except maybe her.

At Broadway/Lafayette I adjust my cock—finally, finally—as she shifts and other passengers block our view of each other, then I move to stand above her, holding onto the rail. She doesn't look up. The train pulls into the station and I place my card in her book. She looks up, startled, and I get that amazing view of her eyes, the one I was waiting for, peering under her long dark lashes, open and big and I could get lost in the way they shimmer. She sees me and blinks.

"In case you want to call me," I say, then step off the train.

I've stopped sweating by the time I get to the bar. My cell rings while I order my first Jameson rocks.

"Hello?"

"Well, if it isn't Sinclair Sexsmith."

No caller ID. Could it be her? It's obviously her. I gulp. Does she know me? It must be her. So soon? "Yes, who's this?"

"Jane," she says. "On the D train. I thought I saw you notice me."

"… You were impossible to miss."

I can almost hear her blush. "Are you busy tonight?" she says.

"Out with friends at the moment, but I could be free later," I say.

"Good. Come join me at the bar on 24th and 10th. 10pm. Alright?"

"… Alright." Why would I argue?

*

The bar is nearly empty, low lights and a few single patrons at the dark counter, quiet. Some low music is coming from somewhere, soft and subtle and electronic. The bartender is polishing pint glasses and laughing low with a woman in red, candles reflected in the glass as she polishes.

"Hey," I say as I approach the bar, making eye contact with the bartender. "Can I get a Jameson rocks?"

She nods, but continues to wipe the glasses. I shoot her a puzzled look. She nods again—a gesture this time, I catch it, she's directing me to look behind me.

I turn and she's there. Jane. Same white wrap dress, same long legs and strappy sandals, same gorgeous dark eyes. She's sipping a martini. A smile on her face like she's amused. She has a second glass on her table: whiskey. On the rocks. Ready for me.

I take one, two, deliberate steps to her table. Place both my palms on it and lean over her, still standing, so she has to look up at me.

I tip my chin to the drink. "That for me?"

She swallows, holding back a smile like she's the cat who got the canary, and nods. Almost nervous, but she's covering it well. She's so sexy with her tiny little movements, fingertips on the glass, looking at me shyly from the side. I don't believe she's queer. No, that's not it—I don't believe she's the kind of femme who primarily sleeps with women. Yet. She picked me up, sure, but I'm beginning to fear I'm her experiment. Maybe she's just a fan—but then again, so what? So maybe she knows what I like—am I being taken by the ways femme can undo me? Am I so preoccupied by her smooth legs (oh my hands on her ankles running up to her knees), her big eyes (looking up like she could swallow me), that I become willing? I'm a sucker sometimes. I'm skeptical. This girl clearly knows how to wield her power.

I keep eye contact for just a flicker, say "thank you," sit down, and take a sip.

*

"I changed it," she's saying. "It's my middle name, really. My grandmother's. My mom is a second-waver, gave me one of those gender-neutral names I always hated. But I never was a girly girl until I started dating butches."

She leans in, as if telling me a secret. My second Jameson is melted ice and she's halfway through her second martini. "I grew up a tomboy, I have three brothers. I mean, I was the bully on the playground! I begged my parents to let me play T-ball and little league like my brothers did. I was the only girl in the league, for a while. Others came after me. My first girlfriend in high school, we met on my softball team. I know, so gay."

We laugh. I knock the ice around in my glass. High school girlfriend. Duly noted.

"I used to dress up for dances and stuff and get made fun of so much. 'Hey, I thought you were gay!' So I put my dresses away. Tried to fit into the lesbian uniform." Jane shrugged, fingering the speared olives in her glass, leaned back again. "But, Sin, seriously—once I finally took my real gender out of the closet, it's been adolescence all over again. New desires, new awakenings. I feel like a teenager." The tip of her toes brush against my ankle.

"Is that so." I lean in, catch her gaze; her eyes are alight.

"'Femme is knowing what you're doing,'" she says, looking down into her drink, then giving me a penetrating stare. "Isn't that how you say it?"

She's quoting me. I was quoting someone else when I wrote that, but either way, I feel trapped and visible and it makes me squirm. She gulps the martini, the liquid too much for her mouth, and chokes a little, sputters, then smiles and wipes her mouth with the back of her hand. My cock stirs.

"C'mon," she says, and gets up.

*

Her place is nearby. It's why she chose that bar—to interview me before taking me home. She planned the whole thing. Those were her best lines back there. She wants me, and she's willing to work for it. I like that.

She locks the door behind us, positioning herself next to me, taking a few steps like it's a dance and she's leading so I follow, and then my back is against the door and she's sighing and flipping her hair and waiting for me to kiss her.

So I do.

She tastes like cream. Smooth, just a tiny bit of thickness, mostly ease and softness. She waits for me to guide her. To show her how I like to be kissed. She doesn't rush in and thrust her tongue, just makes herself warm, wet, open, available.

I let desire increase slowly. Start soft as I get a grip on her hips, her lower back cradled in my forearm, fingers eagerly pulling at the thin fabric of her dress. She lets it get stronger in me, slides her ankle against my calf as she wraps one leg around mine low. I start growling a little, that ravaging tone that is not quite a moan, but a hunger, building.

She arches her back, gasps, cries out, leans into me like she's nuzzling, and starts laughing, delighted. "Fuck," she says and looks at me, catches my gaze, then gets shy and looks down. She fingers my buckle.

"Unbuckle your belt?" she says. And I take it back—that's her best line.

I do, swiftly, pulling the button open, popping the fly, taking my cock out as she kneels, knees wide and pelvis tilted like she's already on top of me and easing down on something big.

She takes me in her mouth tentatively at first, just the head, wraps one hand around it, gauging the length. Can she swallow it all? She's thinking. She laps her tongue, runs her lips down the shaft, then draws a breath and swallows me whole. It's too much for her mouth and she makes a little gulping sound, choking a little. Her smoky eyes water and she looks up at me, keeping it in her mouth. I fight the urge to thrust in again. I can feel the tight O of her throat clenching and she tries to get hold of her gag reflex, then pulls her mouth off and puts her hand back. She rocks her pelvis a little as she sucks, the pretty white fabric of her dress between her knees is falling open and I want my fingers there, want to hear her gasp and oh and yes.

Goddamn she feels good.

She keeps hold of my cock at the base, keeps it pressed against me so I can feel everything. She works it good, pressure and speed and—oh god—I'm going to burst in her mouth. My hands in her hair, on the back of her head. Her gorgeous smoky eyes are smudged and she looks even more beautiful.

I love it when they start to dishevel. Makes me want to tangle her hair, pull at her dress, smear what's left of her lipstick.

*

"Fuck me," she whispers, a command, a request, a desperate need, as she pulls me on top of her on the bed and wraps her legs around the backs of my thighs. I drag my palm from her knee up under her dress and push it aside, tear at the tie and it falls away in one neat cascade of fabric. She nuzzles into my neck again, arms around my shoulders as she sucks my earlobe into her mouth and flicks it with her tongue.

I groan. Fuck. Exposing her skin I take her all in, tracing my gaze along her body, her curvy waist and soft belly, round breasts, small but thick, a handful, cherry nipples and no bra. I catch one in my mouth and encircle the other with my hand. She arches her back, sighs a little, taking a breath in and leaning back, her mouth open, eyes closed, hands at my shoulders, gasping.

I lift up to kiss her. Her mouth supple again and she's eager, open. I'm hard and a little fierce, desire honed and sharpened and ready. Her noises are muffled by my mouth.

I bring my hand to the back of her neck and take hold of a fistful of hair. A gamble with some girls, but Jane wants to be taken, I can feel it. She responds immediately, like a cat does to a stroke of its back, arching and curling into the touch of a hand. Eyes closed, she's taking it in. A gasp and she's still, waiting. I keep my grip. I drag my other fingers down the side of her body, gently, and her nerves are increased from the immobility. She shivers but does not squirm. Waiting.

My hand at her stomach, on top of her thigh, pushing her legs open. I smile. I'm smug in these moments, I can almost start laughing from the waves of power and dominance and pleasure. Go ahead, try me. Go ahead, give in. I'll take you, I'll catch you. I'll make you. Come.

I cup her pussy with my hand and drag my fingers along her lips from on top of her sweet smooth panties, I can feel the outline and she's swollen. She unhinges her hips and spreads them wide, but I need them together so I can slide her panties off. I twist and pull and toss them aside, pull her up by the wrists so I can push the dress from her shoulders, expose her fully.

My mouth on her clavicle, her skin sweet and smooth.

"Please," she whispers, airy, her breath hot. "Please."

I nearly laugh aloud, nearly chuckle, something strong moving deep in me, grinning and restraining myself. I push her gently back down, grab at my cock with my hand.

She reaches for it, lifts her head and shoulders and her stomach flexes. She licks her lips, looks at me. My eyes are on my cock, pushing at my jeans, peeling back the split around the zipper so it doesn't obstruct. It's a silicone cock, just boiled, and doesn't need a condom. I find her cunt with two fingers, my thumb along the shaft, and she's wet, eyes begging for it, waiting, mouth open, jaw tight, one hand behind her on the bed, grabbing at the blankets and waiting for me, breathing in, trying not to growl or scream or hit me, trying not to roll right off the bed and run with all the energy buzzing under her skin right now.

"So sweet," I murmur, tip of my cock touching her cunt. "So, so sweet."

She's tight, I can feel her contract, thick, around me as I slide in. Slowly, slowly. I get to the base and extend my torso, she's watching me and I capture her mouth in a kiss as I slide out. Softly, softly. She adjusts her hips. We are quiet. Sounds of breath and bodies. Her brown eyes are smokier than ever, big and open with flecks of gold that catch the light and I swear I can see myself reflected as she gives me the shyest smile.

"Oh—oh—fuck," she says just under her breath. She leans her head back and her neck is long, stretched, as I pull out quicker, slam back inside.

"More—" she gasps, commanding. "More." Right in my ear, a whisper. I shudder, work in her faster.

"Goddamn," I mutter, a little breathless, my dick swelling and I can feel how she tightens. Her legs around my waist now. Pressing hard against me with resistance, friction.

She bites my shoulder. Claws into my upper back with her hands and I take a sharp breath in, like a splash of cold water, a sudden sharp sensation.

And it's there again, that urge to laugh, to chuckle low as I regain my breath and control. I take hold of her hair again, position my arm across her chest so I'm holding her down and lift myself to my knees, legs apart and slid under her hips. I get the angle just right. Low and tight. A little room to wiggle and the strap of my harness is hitting my clit just right.

This goddamn girl is going to make me come.

She can feel the shift in me and her eyes widen, gaining a look of intensity, concentration, focus. So much effort, so much work, to let someone in, to trust a stranger to hold you up, even your dirty, dark, private places. I want to. I want to be able to catch her, I feel she's falling into some other space and her stomach contracts, she clenches everything as I thrust in, and again, and again, until finally it is precisely right, that one perfect spot and pressure and we are both unraveled, bursting, shaking at the seams, simultaneously, all at once, then shuddering, shaking, gasping, reveling in each other's bodies, and in our own.

"So," Jane says after a moment, low murmurs in her throat, happy sounds of quiet satisfaction, satiation, saturation. "Indian or Thai?"

"Thai," I say. My hand traces lazy circles on her hip, over her skin, delicate as lace.

She kisses me, soft again, supple and deep, and gets up to make the call. She doesn't ask me what I want. She pulls on a robe that barely covers her ass and winks at me as she leaves the room. I tuck my cock into my pants and tidy my perfectly messy hair.

She returns to the bedroom with another whiskey rocks and a glass of white wine, replaces the phone on the nightstand and opens the curtain on her bedroom window, revealing a sliding glass door. She opens it and gestures to me; I follow. It is a lovely view of 10th avenue, a dozen floors up, and we watch the traffic. I marvel at the quiet when I am just above the city.

The quiet is a little long and I should say something. I open my mouth.

"So, Sinclair," says Jane. "Where are you from?"

I grin, and take a sip of the whiskey, so smooth, and the mouthful goes down easy.

The Worst in Me

At first I'm trying to ignore her. I have a new smut collection to read, *Best Lesbian Bondage Erotica*; I have my iPod on to some soothing lofi mix a friend made for me; I have lube in my pocket for a quick jerk-off session before we arrive in New York. I need all the sanctuary and release I can get before returning to that hyper-stimulating city.

But she's making a big show of her many bags, heavy, designer luggage, and she—being a tiny petite thing—seems unable to slip them all into the overhead luggage rack.

The only other person in this car is a man in the back who has been snoring since I got on. I think about telling her to just leave her suitcases on the seat next to her, but her jaw is set, her sensuous mouth twisted in a sneer, and as she begins to climb onto the train seat to reach the rack better, I sigh and, reluctantly, get up to help her.

"Please. Let me," I say, sliding behind her and putting my hand on her waist to guide her out of the way, then taking the heavy suitcase out of her struggling grip and nudge it onto the metal rack easily. She's got a great ass in those tight jeans. Her eyes are wide, then she drags her gaze along my arm to my face. I watch her watch me. She looks like Penelope Cruz, all dark hair and big pools of dark liquid eyes.

"Um," she says. "Thank you."

"Don't mention it," I answer, a bit dismissively, now offering my hand so she can get down. The train doors buzz and are about to close, we'll be in motion shortly. I pick up her other bags and one by one put them up into the rack above her seat. She takes off her thin white sweater and sets it with her handbag next to her, and watches me.

I groan a little with the weight of the last one. She notices. "Thanks again," she says, and I detect a slight accent, French maybe, though she looks Spanish. Her words are a little airy, already pulling Vogue Milan out of her purse and turning her attention to it, a tiny sideways glance at me to see if I'm still standing next to her, waiting for my good-dog biscuit.

I retreat back to my aisle seat. We are facing each other, opposite sides of the train. She is absorbed in her magazine. I put my feet up and crack open my book, start reading through the bondage stories. She takes out a compact and lipstick and fusses with her mouth, repainting, touching her fingertips to the edges of her lips, then wipes microscopic flecks with a tissue. I don't watch her, but she periodically sweeps her eyes over to me. I rest my hand on my neat little package as I read through the story by Toni Amato, "A Girl Like That:" *"She's the kind of girl who brings out the worst in me. Coming on all hip and cool and all into sex, rubbing some part of herself all up against me every chance she gets. ... She makes the worst part of me want to do the best it knows how to teach her a thing or two about fucking."*

I'm stroking my cock unconsciously through my jeans when I notice someone looming next to me, and it's her, she's returning from the bathroom with a clutch in her hand, I didn't even notice her get up. The girl smiles, almost, and pushes past as though I am taking up the entire aisle, or maybe to show off her gorgeous ass in those tight, tight jeans.

The train lurches and opens its sleepy doors, the man in the back of our train car is moving at half-speed and makes his way off the train.

We're alone.

She notices too. She's looking out the window but keeps stealing glances at me. The conductor comes through and says nothing to either of us, just takes the small pieces of paper on our seats, the remnants of our tickets.

I go back to my book. I finger the bottle of lube in my pocket and think this would be a good time to go rub one out, then get absorbed in a story about a dyke cop who is passing as male in a straight club, picks up a girl and takes her, handcuffed, out to her truck. I nearly reach my hand into my pants.

"Um, excuse me?"

She's standing, still in her seat but leaning forward over the seat in front of her, facing me, ass tipped to the side, front of her button down revealing creamy skin, long dark hair swinging. She smiles when I look up, flashes me an intentional smirky pose that she has practiced in the mirror—her seduction look. "Would you help, I have to … I need … something from that bag." She glances up at it.

I put my book down and tug at my jeans to cover my hard-on. Clear my throat. "Sure."

I get up and move toward her. She kneels and reaches for it, her back to the aisle as I come up behind her and reach up.

"This one?" My mouth is close to her ear.

"No, not—yes, that one," she says as I touch the smaller suitcase. She reaches up to help me, bending slightly forward, as we both ease the weight of her bag down onto the seat. And I swear she rubs right against me, pushing back, just a little. Maybe I'm imagining it. Yeah, sure Sinclair; you just happen to have a boner and this girl offers up her ass on a silver platter.

I back off. Return to my seat. Again.

"Um, thanks!" she calls.

I toss a half-smile over my shoulder. "Don't mention it." She pulls a bundle of fabric out of her bag and I don't watch. I don't pay attention. I can't see it. I shouldn't be watching, but I am. It is slinky and red. She finds a few other bits and tucks her hair behind her ear, gathers an armful of clothing, makes her way toward me, down the aisle, to the bathroom at the back of the car.

She's in there a while. I try to concentrate on my book, to not wonder what she is doing, what she's slipping into, who she's meeting when she gets off the train, not to imagine being that somebody so filled with lust and permission that I'd fuck her right on the platform, couldn't even control myself long enough to wait until we went to dinner, drinks, a show, whatever it is she's dressing up for. My breath is quickening and my hands are starting to do that aching thing where they are pulsing with grip, wanting to hold push grab press punch slap.

She makes her way back to her seat like the aisle is a runway, like she's coming in for a landing. Each step deliberately placed. Legs precisely angled and separated and her gait is sharp, strong. Her red dress swings from her hips, past her thighs, to her knees. A few bracelets jangle from one arm, simple and slim. She's pulled her hair up high on her head, into some sort of ponytail, then twisted around itself in a beautiful knot.

I watch her as she closes the distance to her own seat. I don't drool. I am not drooling. I try not to drool at the sight of her ankles, her calves, the hints of the backs of her knees as her dress swings. I wipe my mouth. Her ankles cross just slightly, which makes her hips curl and switch like a figure eight. Like a come-hither finger.

I swallow. Breathe in. And quickly open my book, flustered, and turn it to the page I was reading as she slides onto the train seat and I snap out of my spell.

Of course—of course—I am too zealous and the book slides out of my hand, skittering out into the aisle. I take a sharp breath in and some spit goes down the wrong way, I start to choke, cough, loudly, as I jump up to retrieve the book.

Oh good lord. I get ahold of myself. Straighten up, book in hand. Clear my throat. I don't look at her. I can't see her. I am sure I am five shades of crimson and I steal a glance her direction, she's covering her mouth, that perfect smirky smile, eyes dancing, looking away from me. Obviously she saw everything.

Fuck.

I resettle. Book in lap, adequate breath in lungs. I sneer to myself. Re-open the erotica. *Do you have to be so obvious?* I yell at myself in my head. *You dumbass. Real smooth, Sexsmith.*

She's going through her open case next to her, I can see her arms moving but can't see what she's doing. Then suddenly she's up, out of the seat and back in the aisle, pads down toward me as if she forgot something.

I catch a whiff of her perfume as she walks by. Dizzying, intoxicating. The swish of her skirt. I watch her little toe-heel trot down the aisle. My body acts without my mind and I reach for her. My hand on her hip. Lightly at first, but then she doesn't pull away and I grab her harder. Both hands and I stand, pull her toward me, her back to me, and she is still. I can't see her face but I can feel her breath through my hands, she's holding it. Surprised. Waiting.

I lift her skirt in the back to reveal her perfect ass. A

work of art. A combination of genetics and squats and hundreds of hours at the gym. She knows it. She's bare under her red dress, no panties, no stockings. Perhaps that's what she forgot. I can't resist, I palm the apple of her ass, caress the flesh, spreading her cheeks and opening her slit.

She lets out her breath, finally, and it comes with a breathy moan, just a little.

And I'm gone. The slightest noise from her lips and all I can feel is what it'll be like to be inside her, to feel her body curl around my arm and buck and thrash and grasp as she comes. I've got to feel it. Got to make her.

I press against her back. Her neck is bare, hair up, and my mouth is just at the corner of her jaw, below her ear. I reach around her and pin her arms to her sides, pressing her back to lean against me, and she arches, thrusts her hips up, feels the cock behind my fly. She lets her head lean back against me, lets me take her weight.

"Bend over." Right next to her ear. Barely audible.

I release her from my hold. She turns her head just a bit and her face is quizzical, open, lustful, a tad resistant. I run my hand up under her dress firmly, continue to drag it up her back, then press, hard, on her shoulder blades, bending her over the train seat in front of her.

"I said bend over."

Faster now. Unbuckle and unzip. The dress pushed up to her waist, one hand on her lower back to keep her hips tipped up to me. Her asshole is dark pink, a burst between her cheeks, perfectly smooth, and her ass is perfectly round, my thighs are already quivering and hips pulsing, so ready to fuck.

I grab one of the condoms I always keep tucked into the inner pocket of my bag. Roll it on. Spit into my palm, and again, lube up my cock. Spit again at my two fingers and shove them at her hole.

I hear her gasp—"ah"—just once—and she glances back over her shoulder, eyes heavy-lidded and dark. I push on her upper back again.

"Head down."

Her body shudders at my voice and gives in. A ripple of submission through her backbone and I feel to my toes the way it makes every hair on my body stand up, clench, awaken.

Cockhead at her asshole, I enter her easily, so smooth. So tight. The resistance of her ass is just more friction and tension between us and I want to tear into her. Split her apart. Harder now. Faster and she's taking it so well. "So fucking good," I whisper to myself. It's so good. She keeps her legs strong and pushes back against me. It's not enough lube and I remember the bottle in my pocket and laugh to myself. What kind of pervert am I to carry lube on the train?

I pull out and squirt it right on my dick, smear it, and ease back into her.

Fuck yes, give me that ass. Give it to me.

The girl in the red dress has her arms braced against the seats, bracelets jangling. We hit a rhythmic sliding stride and she brings her forearm down in front of her, leans forward, brings her other hand between her legs. Immediately I feel her knees weaken and press together, back arch and spine curl and oh it's beautiful. I bring my hand up her spine to her shoulder blades, then her neck, take a handful of hair and keep her steady. She pulls against me, not to get away, but to heighten sensation. Struggling has such varying degrees. She doesn't want out, she wants more.

I take grips on her hip and hair. Slam against her hard, pull out slow. Slick where my cock is fat inside her, swelling and eager. Resistance and tension. She tips even further forward onto the seat until she's held up by it, lifted at the waist, hand furious between her legs, thighs pressed so hard together, on her tiptoes straining up and tipping forward more, further, until she lets one foot come up off the floor and bend at the knee, toes curling.

She is starting to let go, really let go, become undone at the seams, and she can't keep the tension in her muscles so she stops resisting my hand in her hair, my palm against the flesh of her ass, holding her cheeks apart, fingers gripping her hipbone. But I don't let go, I just hold her stronger, tighter, take her a little deeper as she opens, opens deeper, opens hard, and every hinge in her body loosens, I feel it from inside pulse and ripple and again, and again, until she is gasping, chest heaving, crying out, gasping for air. And I ease up, slide in slow, press hard and sweet against her as her orgasm fades, shudders, and her body rebuilds itself anew.

I pull out and let her rest. We are quiet a moment. I release my hand from her mess of hair and caress her neck gently, let my hand drape across her hips and thighs, even find her hand, wet and warm from her own liquid, touch her fingertips gently.

Her breathing calms. She sighs, once. Reaches up to brush her hair from her face and I stand, tuck my cock, zip up, run my fingers through my perfectly messy hair to assess the damage.

She stays where she is, leaning for support over the bench seat. I pull the skirt of her dress down over her hips with a shit-eating grin on my face and smack her ass once, a little harder than I meant to, but playful, and she gasps and tenses, then stands. Her makeup is smeared. Her face is still open and sweet from the release but it changes as she watches me. I gather my book and pocket bottle of lube and put them back in my bag, pick up my jacket and slide my arms into the sleeves.

She's still watching. Eyes wide. Breathing.

"We're here," I say. The train is slowing and I can just

make out the tunnels of Penn Station as we arrive in New York City. She blinks. Opens her mouth to say something.

I grin. Lord she's cute. I kiss her cheek as I slip by her and remove her heavy suitcases from the overhead racks. I notice strappy black high heel shoes at her seat and my mouth waters.

Heaving the last of the bags down, I turn to her again. She's still by my seat, now empty, one finger in her mouth, looking a little shy. I smile and nod, once, a goodbye-take-care-have-a-nice-night gesture, and turn to the door as the train comes to a full stop.

"Um!" she calls after me. I look back. "Thank you?"

I give her a long glance from her ankles up to her legs to her hips and belly and breasts, the disheveled red dress, hair tumbling from its neat design on her head. She's stunning, really. Delicious.

"Don't mention it," I say, and step off the train.

All Five Senses

It starts in the Brooklyn library, the back row, the classics section; the air so thick with ink and brittle paper and crumbling paste. I pick up a worn leather copy of *Antigone*, its cover so oiled down with decades of fingers and hands opening, turning its pages, breaking its spine. So soft it feels like suede.

I sit on the industrial carpet and flip it open, easily absorbed: Nothing painful is there, nothing fraught with ruin, no shame, no dishonor, that I have not seen in thy woes and mine.

When I look up, a few minutes later, there she is: sitting on the floor in a row I can hardly see, at first she is only visible by her bare legs on the dirty carpet, seated like I am on the floor, knees all bent, one tucked under her gray skirt which is a small mess of cover for her thighs. I slowly shift my body further into the aisle. Her back is to me, and she holds up a mirror in front of her—I catch glimpses of her face reflected. The dark, nerdy frames of her glasses, the line of her jaw, her chin, then her mouth.

She takes out a tube of lipstick, twirls it erect, and paints the perfect outline of her lips. Slow, real slow. She presses them together and presses them forward in a kiss, makes an O with her mouth and touches just the tip of her finger to the edge.

I hold my breath.

I find my hand brought up to my face without really noticing. Pads of my fingers against the butch stubble on my chin, I didn't shave this morning, I didn't think I'd need to, and now the tiny hairs are strong as teeth and my fingertips are burned with the day-old five o'clock shadow. I watch the soft, smooth pillow of her lips over her shoulder in the mirror. I imagine smearing that lipstick across her cheek with my thumb, hard enough that the trail of red would feel like it was made without paint.

Carpeting scratching at the palms of my hand, I'm leaning so far forward that if I was in a movie, this is the moment I would knock over a pile of books and she'd look up at the crash. Instead, I feel a tickle in my nose and the ink and paper and dust smell is suddenly amplified. I scurry back to my small stack of collected books and satchel, but I don't get to my handkerchief in time, and I let out a strong sudden sneeze.

"Bless you," I hear, softly, from across the aisle. I can hear each letter in her words. I imagine the way her red mouth looks forming the shapes of the sounds.

I swallow, blow my nose gently, mumble, "Thanks." I don't look back over to her, but go back to the library stacks, sifting through the Dewey decimal numbers on the spines, fingering the worn covers, the different textures, letting my fingers stroke the books as I take a few steps and follow the books around the corner.

Soon I'm in the next aisle from her. I can see right through it and I try to justify that I'm here looking for books, classics, something to support a recent article's thesis that there were some butch/femme roles for women in ancient

Greece and Rome. The library is so quiet, I can hear when she shifts on the floor, still reading, now with her back to the stacks of books and both feet on the floor, knees bent and separated, short skirt sliding up her thighs.

I'm going to get caught, I know it.

But it is as if hands are pressing on my shoulders and I sink lower, eyes wide, praying my knees won't creak or pop as I crouch, strain my eyes to get a look at her thighs. I quickly grab a big picture book out of the stack to flip through, to cover up my voyeurism.

She's pinching her dark brown hair that is falling over her shoulder between thumb and forefinger, swirling her fingers around it, twisting. I see her eyes darting across the page of the book she's holding in her other hand, the cover against her thighs. I can't tell what the book is, but it looks modern, it does not live in the dust of the classics section, it is paperback and skinny.

She glances to where I just was and sees my small stack of books, but she lost track of me. Her eyebrows curl for just a moment, and she glances around the other direction but there's no one there either. We're alone—she thinks she's alone. I hold my breath and try not to move. I know it's voyeuristic of me, but she is in public. She must know someone could possibly see her. That must be part of the thrill.

She shifts, knees together, pulls her feet closer to her body, and I catch the sight of her simple white cotton panties between her legs, thin, so thin I can nearly see through them. She pushes her skirt up her thighs just a bit farther and slides her hand into them. The fabric strains.

Her fingers move slowly and she keeps her eyes on the pages of the book. Clearly a good one, I wonder what she's reading, if its contents are queer or kinky, if she's thinking about the taste of sweat and salty skin, the sounds of moans that emerge out of places where bodies collide, the sight of a fist disappearing at the wrist, the sting of an open-palm smack on the ass or cheek or cunt, the scent of desire, like musk, like the ocean, like a fertile ground.

Her fingers move faster. Hair falls into her eyes and her jaw drops open just a little. (Really, this is really happening?) Her lips pinken, eyelids flutter as her eyes dart across the page. Her strong thighs are quivering a little and I can see if I fucked her she'd want them pressed together, bent deep at the hips. It's the way her knees want to close but her hand is in the way.

My hand goes to my zipper. (Should I?) Hard packing today, as I often do on weekends, just for me, to feel the weight and bulk between my legs, the strain of the seam of my jeans. No one has to know, no one usually does; just a private, personal experience between me and my cock. I run my finger down the shaft of it, through my jeans, remember its girth as I watch her bite her lip, hand still moving slow and vigorous between her legs. I thumb the head, the little ridge, catch it in the instep of my hand between thumb and forefinger. I get enough of a grip to press it back into my clit and start pulsing against it.

I feel a stab of guilt and fight the impulse to unbuckle, unzip. Nearly unbearable. I can barely breathe.

She's getting lost in the sensations, spreading from her pelvis to her thighs and belly and down and up. Her breathing is getting faster, hand is faster between her legs, fingers working her clit, I can see through the thin white cotton through the stacks of books. She leans her head back and closes her eyes entirely, lets the book start to slip from her lap as her thighs squeeze and close and she presses her hips forward. I have a perfect visualization of how her back would arch if she was on her stomach on my bed, ass in the air, thighs and knees strong together, my own hand buried in her cunt.

I stroke my own cock harder and feel my breath quicken to match hers. She's gasping as she breathes in, I can hear her. I watch her hips buck, face flushing, as she comes in a quiet flourish, calm and sudden, eyes closed, head bent back. She brings her fingers to her lips and sucks, then opens her eyes, looking straight forward for the first time, right at me.

Panic. Does she see me? She glances right back down to her book as her eyelids flutter and adjusts her skirt and glasses, gives herself a minute to catch her breath, picks up her book and purse, and, slightly wobbly on her feet, leaves the classics section.

I let out a breath, lean back against the stacks, take my hand out of my pants, zip up, and head toward the checkout.

It's nearly dark outside by the time I gather all my things and make it through the line. I finger the spines of the books and flip my wallet in the palm of my hand, remembering my cock just minutes before, thinking of this girl and her strong legs, swift fingers.

That should've been the end of that.

But ten minutes later, picking up take-out extra-hot red curry at my favorite Thai place, I hear behind me: "Well, well."

I turn. It's her. Of course it's her. How did we end up at the same place? She's three inches shorter than me and wearing heels. Her cheeks are flushed from the chilly weather and I notice her lipstick, remember watching her redden her mouth. Does she know I watched her? Does she know me? Did she see me that whole time?

She's looking at me, but she can't be. I don't know her. I glance to my left and right and nearly do that stupid pointing to my chest and mouthing, "*Me?*" when she giggles a little, and takes a step toward me, outstretches her hand. "I'm Juliet."

I clear my throat and take her hand. "Sinclair." I try not to look flustered.

"I usually do this kind of thing in the other order, but hey, I give you points for originality," Juliet says, eyes shining, and shimmies by me to the counter to pay for her take-out and mine, leaving me aghast. I recover a moment too slowly and say, "No, please, let me ..." fumbling with my wallet, but she's waving her hand at me dismissively and shoots me a look over her shoulder that says *back the fuck off, I got this*, so I do.

I'd planned on taking my curry home but she carts our two trays to an empty table and sets them both down, gets up to fetch silverware, and glances at me expectantly. I can't find my voice and sit across from her, stunned, as she folds her napkin in her lap, arranges her food, and takes a few bites.

"So what're your books for? For fun? Or are you doing research?" She reaches for her water and shoots me a smile.

I open my mouth but nothing comes out. She's so damn articulate, and speaks quickly, boldly, which catches me off guard. I pick up my fork and mix my curry and rice on my plate—not really date food, so strong and long-lasting in the body, but—is this exactly a date? Not really. I still can't form the words to answer her question. What was her question again? I take a bite of the red curry and it explodes in my mouth: at first it's just hot but then the subtle layers of the curry hit my palette and I taste sweet coconut milk, basil, bay leaves. Strong and bold. My lips tingle with the heat of the spice. I take a sip of water and look up at Juliet; she's chewing slowly, waiting for me to say something. I swallow.

"I was looking for evidence of butch/femme roles in antiquity cultures," I start, finally comprehending what she'd asked me.

She nods, takes another bite of her curry, green, and

listens as I tell the story of the play I saw a few months back, the Oedipus Cycle in full, and how it struck me that women's roles may have varied more than represented in the typical Greek canonical texts. I'm not an antiquity scholar—at all—but I do study gender, so I got inspired to re-read some of the most famous works with an eye toward gender theory.

We chat on and on. The conversation is fantastic; a perfect combination of asking questions, answering, and listening to each other. She is new to New York and moved here to be with a girl; but the move promptly broke them up. Meanwhile she's working in a bank, she wants to go to business school, she loves Thai food, she's 28, born and raised in Minneapolis.

She starts to tell me her femme story as I am finishing my curry. My mouth is aflame and this conversation is the best I've had in months, I've nearly forgotten what it's like to be charmed by a pretty girl's first date version of her life story, such a fascinating character study falls into place.

We're done eating, but she's still telling her femme story. It's like a coming out story—we all have one, we all have the struggle to understand and then the eventual development and acceptance of our own sexual and gender orientations. I'm actively listening, watching her eyes dance, watching her lips and teeth, her hands as she illustrates her points with gesticulation.

She takes her lipstick out of her bag and uncaps it, twists it up and paints her mouth subtly, softly. A gesture I remember well and which stirs something in me.

I take advantage of her momentary pause in the story. I want to hear more about her life. I lean in toward her on my elbows and catch her eye, give her a hard stare. "Can I walk you home?"

She stops, considers, and puts her lipstick away. "That'd

be great," she says, holding my gaze a moment longer, then begins to gather her things. "Now? Shall we?"

I nod, stand and put on my coat, grab my satchel, clear off our plastic trays and take-out containers. Not exactly a smooth date ... but the sight of those thin white cotton panties under her grey skirt keeps flashing in my mind and I want to feel her, want to fuck her, want my hands under her skirt, up her thighs, on her tits.

Her apartment, it turns out, is not far from my favorite curry place. We walk the few long blocks slowly, strolling, savoring each other's company. She takes my elbow, submissive, but leads the way, keeping close to me with an occasional dip of her head into my neck and shoulder as she keeps telling the story of herself, sweet, so sweet, and unselfconscious.

At her stoop we're still talking. I'm opening up a little about my gender, my history, my character. I'm in storytelling mode, all melodrama and timing, and she's watching my face, sitting on her very New York stoop as I have one foot up on the low stair, telling her how I came to be where I'm at. Her eyes are sparkling, hands together in her lap.

We laugh. It's one of those perfect conversations where I'm charming with awkward real moments without trying. I don't want this date to end.

Neither does she. "Coming up?" she asks, as if we're already lovers, standing and slowly stepping up the stairs, looking back over her shoulder as she opens her purse for keys.

I grin, and follow her in.

The moment she closes the door behind me she gives me a look that tells me exactly what I need to know: she's done chatting. I take my jacket off and she steps next to me to take it, then tosses it onto the hallway chair and presses me swiftly against the wall, her arms next to my head.

I smile, hands reflexively going to her hips. "Oh, is that what you think." It's not a question. We haven't even kissed yet. Our mouths are nearly touching. She grinds up against me, my thighs between hers, and I can tell she knows I'm packing.

"Who packs to the library?" she asks, softly, in my ear, hot breath on my neck.

I shrug, a little sheepish, exposed. "Me," I say, and get a grip around her waist to quickly switch places with her, press her up against the wall, and lower my mouth onto hers.

The first kiss: oh it gives away so much. The way she tastes, the way she sounds when she breathes, whether she keeps her eyes open, what sounds she makes, whether she claws at me with her hands or wraps her legs around me or feather-touches my face. All the senses activated, heightened. Such sensation. Plus: the power she keeps is all revealed. Will she let me take, let me lead, let me control? Give over her strength while she begs and submits?

Juliet's kisses are insistent, fierce, fiery. I let her lead a while and get a sense of her style, then stop her quick to push my thighs between hers and press my forearm to her breastbone against the wall. She nearly growls, lets out a low hummed breath, and allows herself to be restrained, enjoys the feeling of restriction.

"When did you know I was packing?" I say, my mouth close to hers.

"When you walked through the reference section."

I consider the timeline: before I hit Classics. Just after I walked in. She brings her mouth to mine and lets me work through this in my mind. That means she followed me to Classics. That means she put on that little show on purpose. Does she know I saw her? Probably. I grin, amused. If she didn't know I was there, she secretly hoped I was.

I'll take it either way.

She watches my face as I work through this and knows she's been found out, knows I saw her. She waits for me to get it, then a smirky little self-satisfied smile plays over her lips, like something is very funny, like the joke's on me, and I get the strong urge to slap her, bring my palm to her cheek fast and wipe that smirk from her face, watch her gasp and look back to me wide-eyed.

I don't. I don't even know her, I wouldn't want to be rude. But when I do know her, I will, and she'll like it.

"Really." I say, chewing my tongue and decidedly not slapping her. "So that little show you put on—"

"Oh, you mean with the ... lipstick?" She takes one of my hands in both of hers and brings my index finger to her mouth, making an O of her perfect lips and sliding it in. I feel the soft soft smoothness of her inner lips, the rough scrape of her teeth, the sweetness of her tongue, warm, damp, and then I feel her suck and my eyes roll back in my head.

I groan, audibly (dammit). Goddamn.

She smiles with my fingertip between her teeth, closes her lips, and sucks deep again. She knows now: knows how to have me if she decides she wants to. Knows I like my dick sucked, I'm that kind of guy, knows she can make me weak and take me down with the sweet spot on her tongue.

I can't really take it; I grab her hair. Hard, harder than I mean to but she's got me all worked up already, and I bring my mouth to hers, forceful, and her lips are so supple, sweet, mouth in that tiny O, she lets out the softest muffled gasp and melts a little against the wall, against me.

A thought quickly passes through my mind: I want her to be mine. Where'd that come from? I want to be no one's, I need too much room for that, I won't get lost again. Still, maybe I can have that and have her, too. Something in me warms and smiles at the idea. I already trust her more than I should, and I don't know why, but I like it, and it scares me.

I push the thought away and focus on her mouth. Her arms are up around my neck, hands at the back of my head in the short hairs, tenderly fingering my collar. I arch into it and let myself feel it, really feel it. Her fingers unweave chains of protection I've put there, carefully removing one link at a time.

She lets one hand drift to my zipper and swiftly unbuttons, unzips my fly, pulls out my hard packer. She knows what she's doing. She licks her lips, pulls away from me, sinks to her knees. I leave my hand in her hair. She leaves her glasses on.

Her mouth works on my cock expertly. She is not shy—bold, grinning when she pulls back to use her tongue, licking around the crown and piss slit, working her palm along the shaft, taking the whole thing deep in her mouth, lips shining, slick.

"Ummmm," she gulps and looks up at me, eyes under her glasses. I run my fingers through her short hair, dyke-length but so femme.

She sucks me hard, deep, all the way in, and takes her hands away, unbuttons her creamy low-cut short-sleeved blouse and slips it from her shoulders, down her arms. Her breasts are beautiful, buoyant, more than a handful, her cleavage deep, bra lacy and white. She rises to stand up on her knees, cock still in her mouth, gives me a hard look, a shy twinkle in her eye that makes me chuckle. She slides her lips from my cock and puts her hand there instead, runs her fingers expertly up the shaft, fast, vibrating my cock and my harness with just the right pressure.

I groan. She grins. She's enjoying this. Gives a low laugh as I catch my breath.

"What's so funny," I say, trying to sound demanding,

gripping at her hair and twisting for effect. My knees are weak.

She takes a deliberate look to my cock and back to my face. "I like it," she says quietly, not shy but feigning bashfulness; her glasses have slipped down her nose and she pushes them back up, and I nearly topple over with the arousal.

"C'mon," I straighten up and take a few steps back into her living room, small but comfortable, a touch of elegance, rich colors and fabrics. "To the couch."

I sit and push my jeans down so my cock bobs straight up from my clit, hard and waiting. I put my hand on it, stroke it gently, and look to her.

She doesn't miss a beat, comes right over and kneels between my legs again, topless now, nipples hard, she tosses her bra in her wake, that little grey skirt still swishing at her thighs.

She looks up at me as she takes it in her mouth again. Easy. Like she knows just how it fits. Sucks it all the way down and holds it in her throat. Her hands on my thighs. Sucking hard, getting it nice and wet.

She eases up and moves closer, tall on her knees, and presses her breasts into me, between my legs, against my thighs, before she squeezes them together and slides my cock between them, tongue out and long to lick the tip of my head when it comes up through her cleavage. Fucking her tits, slow, deep.

My eyes roll back but I try to keep watch. Her red red lips, her hands on her breasts, pinching her hard nipples and wide dark areolas. Faster, cock sliding up and down as I thrust my hips against her, she likes that, can tell I am liking this, her eyes fix on my face and she's wondering how I'll fuck her later, how hard my hips can pound, how many times she'll come.

I grin at her, smoky-eyed, voice low. "Dirty girl."

She lets out a soft laugh, pleased. Shifts herself so she's farther under my cock and I feel her breasts against my balls, against my lips, hard, her fingers rolling her nipple as she uses it to trace against my cunt, under my harness, then against the opening, nipple pushing inside just an inch.

She gets hold of my cock with her mouth at the same time and looks up at me, eyes sparkling behind her dark glasses. So dirty! What is she doing to me? This is not what I expected, not anything I ever would've asked for, but oh it feels good. I didn't think I could even feel it like this but her nipple is penetrating, teasing, my dick getting harder in her mouth as she works it up and down, in and out, pressing her tits into me.

"Jesus, you know what you want, don't you," I gasp. It is a thrill to be taken like this. I feel strong, still on top despite my increasingly sensitive cock in her mouth, despite the growing wish that she'd put her fingers inside.

"Mmmhmm," she hums, and I feel the vibration in my dick and clit, her mouth full of me, pressing on her tongue.

"Let me have your fingers," I say, and she looks up at me, glasses falling on her nose so she pushes them up and wraps her hand around the base of my cock, pushing. I groan. Shit that's good. Her nipple barely in my cunt drives my thighs apart, makes me press hard into her. "No, inside," I say. "Do it."

She looks surprised, but complies, sliding two fingers in easily, and I can feel myself slick, tight but relaxing against the pressure she curls onto my g-spot.

Her nipple has easily shifted to my clit. Hard against it, feels almost like her clit against mine, flicking, quickly back and forth while her fingers press at me—gently, gently, not really moving but providing sweet presence, something for me to tighten against from inside.

She looks up at me to check in, check my face, gauge my response, and I'm melting under her touch, trying to keep my big-bad-top persona and still give over to this sensation. I trust her more than I should, maybe, but I like it. It feels good to let her in; it feels honest. I'm supple and her fingers are a hot knife through butter, separating me and letting all my cold resistance go, which in turn lets me harden, tighten, swell in her mouth as she puts my cock back in it, I can feel every inch of her tongue and teeth and lips and I want to come down her throat.

She feels me clench and doesn't let up, takes my cock an inch deeper, flicks her nipple over my clit harder, pushes her fingers against my g-spot, pressing, quivering against her, shaking, clenching tight, so tight the muscles in my calves and ass are starting to pinch and I want to let up but I know I'm close, so close, and she works my cock in and out of her mouth, sounds from how wet her mouth is, faster, and she catches it in her teeth and opens her mouth for air, gasps a little and gulps, catches my eye as she swallows me deep, deeper, I can feel it in the back of her throat, pulsing, closing tight around the head of my cock and my eyes roll back, hands grasping for the pillows on the couch, for her hair, for anything I can get ahold of, and I see stars, and come, squirt hard which I never do, splashing all over her tits as she keeps her nipple hard against my clit. Yelling out in deep moans and grunts, unselfconscious. Shit, I don't even know if she lives alone—I suddenly come to and feel exposed, vulnerable, but she is looking up at me with the sweetest open face, such lust and reverence and respect, and she takes her fingers away from my cunt, puts them back on my cock and holds it, gently, in her hand, as if testing to see how hard I am still, as if asking me not to stop, to keep going.

I clear my throat and sigh a little, take a deep breath.

"You know what I think," I say, running my hands through my hair before I lean forward to pull her to me and kiss her pretty wet mouth. She shakes her head. "You're not a top. Not that that wasn't amazing, god, it was—Juliet. Wow."

She blushes. It's unbelievably cute.

"But I think you know how to submit."

She almost whimpers, bites her lower lip self-consciously and unconsciously, I see her chest heave a little, heart softening. She does. I knew it.

It was daring of her to be so bold with a bj, but I really like that. It forgives me the apology I constantly carry for being a cock-identified lesbian-feminist queer dyke. A butch who fetishizes gender dynamics and craves gendered play in the bedroom—if she wants my cock so bad she's willing to take it, I know it's okay that I want it that bad, too.

Still, I'd told her I was a top. I'd even touched on my flirtation with stone, that I don't crave getting off myself the same way I crave getting a girl off. That sex for me is the most satisfying when I'm in charge, when she is exhausted and satiated from all the fucking. That is my drug, that is the high for which I ache.

And I want that now, want to toss her down and take her, feel her skin, I've barely even had my hands on her, want to run my hands up and under that grey skirt and find out if she comes the way I think she does, clenching her thighs together, she likes to be pounded hard, the muscles in her ass and stomach give that away. Her curvy calves and strong, sure steps in her librarian heels: I can tell she's got muscle.

I like her mouth on mine. She doesn't kiss like a top, that too is part of the clue. She's insistent, and pushes back, matches me, but she gives over and lets go in a way that stirs those dominant demons in my belly and shoulders. I want to hear her gasp and look at me with a little shock, a little fear, waiting for me to hurt her or sooth her or fuck her.

I feel something blossoming between us, and I want to explore it.

I pull her to her feet and rise to mine, stepping out of my jeans. I wrap my arms around her waist, pull her close for a fiercely gentle kiss, feel her breasts against my chest, nipples hard. Running my hands along her skin, feeling her gasp and shudder against me, I find the zipper on her skirt and unhook the latch, let it fall to the floor. She steps out of it, heels and glasses still on, and I loop my fingers under the band of her panties. I kiss her jaw, her neck. She brings her arms around my neck and leans into my mouth, tilts her head to let me taste her. She sighs a little with the sensitivity.

Taking hold of her upper arms in my fists I push them back behind her, spreading her chest open, presenting her tits nicely, while pulling her to me and kissing her mouth again, hard. She gasps, and I harden, feel a low growl rushing. Her kisses leave me breathless.

"Bedroom. Now." I order. "Lead the way."

She looks at me with smoldering eyes. "You have a really sexy voice," she says, soft, breathy, a little higher than her speaking voice, this is her seduction voice, her turned-on vocal chords when her scales are all desire and want.

Leading me into the bedroom is in slow motion: I watch her from behind and see every angle, every curve of her legs as she lifts and steps, every squeeze of her ass, every soft toss of her hair. From here she looks infinitely confident, and I shiver. Top doubt. Am I badass enough to take her down?

Her bedroom is sparse, accented with silver, a heavy mirror opposite the bed with a thick metal frame, glimmering when she hits the lamp on the bedside table. Her duvet is white, accented with stitching in elaborate swirls, pillow cases matching filled with pillows thick and fluffy. The linens make her bed a cloud, all evaporated water and gentle rolling. I bet I like my mattresses harder than she likes hers. The bed frame is silver too, tall bars that swoop at the top in some swirls, a modern design, bars thick and probably cool, perfect for gripping.

I register little in her room other than her bed. She's got it on risers. It is perfectly hip-height.

And then she gives me that look. That look that everyone who has ever fucked a girl (well) has seen, that gorgeous look of desperation and desire, fierce and fiery; that look that might be what Medusa looks like, if anyone ever lived to tell of the power behind her eyes. I can be devoured by that look, I've seen it before and it has unraveled me at the seams. I've seen that look and been destroyed – but not this time. This time I hold her gaze. I let her funnel all the power she can gather right into me, and I take it.

I'm vibrating with the power she's pouring into me, torn between the sweetness of the connection with this beautiful girl and the urge to take her down. That look is deliberate. So much happens in the eyes, so much input, so much seeing. She licks her lips. Watches me as the struggle in me builds, that thin line between taking and losing control.

Fuck it.

I move quickly, arms reaching and body curling before she even registers that I'm lunging for her, all animal instinct and growl, twisting my grip in her hair to turn her body away from me and toss her on her stomach on the bed, she sinks into her cloud and gasps, her body responds immediately, arching her back, ass in the air, white cotton little girl panties still on but wet in the middle, I can see it from here, librarian heels presenting her ass like it's on a pedestal. She turns her head, presses one cheek to the white bedspread, pushes her hair out of her face and looks back at me, glasses askew, trying to catch her breath and breathing in hard.

I rip her panties from her hips, push them down her legs and leave them tangled at her ankles, clinging. She's bent at the waist over the edge of the bed, I stand behind her, cock perfectly poised. Her pussy is slick and tight, thick, swollen. I don't wait. One hand on the curve of the small of her back and pushing her hips up and back, into me, the other hand guiding my cock in swiftly, hard, shoving inside the whole length of it as she moans and opens.

Juliet reaches one hand behind her and pulls on her ass from the side, fingertips just touching the lips of her pussy, so pink next to the whites of her short femme nails. Her mouth is open, back arched, neck arched, hair swinging next to her cheeks as I slide my cock in and out, in and out. She's so slick I don't need lube, so swollen and tight, I feel my cock being milked as she squeezes against me.

She keeps her thighs pinched hard together, which keeps her pussy even tighter. Her clit is thick and hard, I can feel it where my index finger hits her as I keep my hand wrapped around my cock at the base, pushing it in the right place.

"Fuck ... fuck ... fuck," she gasps each time I slam into her.

I'm messing up her perfectly made bed. Crisp corners, smooth folds, linens tucked tight turn me on big time. As if she knew she could be expecting company later. I imagine her bent over, reaching, and pulling the corners down, in her little grey skirt, before she left for the library earlier. It's like a particularly made up-do, delicately balanced with clips and curls, which to me just screams to be torn down in fistfuls, taken down and messed up.

The panties around her ankles are restricting her movement, but she doesn't really want to spread her legs. Keeps them tight and together and she's bucking back into me harder now. Harder, back arching as she grabs at the bedspread and opens her mouth wide, whole body curling, before she lets out a thick moan, shudders, and collapses under me, coming suddenly, hard, thrashing a little on the bed before she quiets.

"Don't stop, don't stop," she starts to plead, as I slow, putting my hands on the curves of her waist and shoulders, soothing soft touches. She puts her hand back on her ass again to spread her pussy apart for me, regains her friction against the bed and grinds her hips back onto my cock again.

It doesn't take much to set me off again. She's even slicker now, I work my hips faster and not as deep, ridges of my cockhead rubbing against her lips as I go in and out. Moving my hand down between her legs again I tip her hips up and back and manage to get her clit under my fingers, hard and swollen, and with just one or two flicks she's coming again, gasping and groaning into the bedspread, gripping her hands at the edge of the bed.

I grin with her release and don't let up. She can take more. I recognize the way she's coming now, in bursts, she's multiply orgasmic and I wonder how many times in a row she can do it. I don't let up my hand on her clit and keep moving it in circles and she comes again, deeper this time, and I don't stop, keep my hand on her, keep her pinched between my cock and fingers as she opens farther and shudders against me, deeper moans coming from her abdomen up and out of her throat.

As her body calms I lean over her, kiss her shoulder, neck, my mouth by her ear. "That was beautiful. But I'm not quite done with you yet."

I back up and pull out fast, a little too fast to be kind, and she gasps, but I reach to get a grip on her arms and pull her back up to standing. She staggers a little with her ankles stuck in her white panties and I steady her as she steps out of them, leaves them on the floor. I pull back the covers, throw the duvet down to the foot of the bed. Then: there is the sound of sheets being pulled back, the snap it makes when the bed has been made so nice and neat. As if pulling the entire structure out of the bed, and its neatness collapses, lines once straight get bent and askew, unhinging the architecture until it is only a poof of linens, snapping back. It reverberates in her silver room.

I glance to her and gesture with a quick jerk of my head. "Up."

She's dazed. Her eyes are glazed. She hears me, lower lip quivers and she wants to move but the desire in her body is stunning her a little, I can see it, thick, around her.

I grab her arm and pull. "Get up here," I say again, more gently, pressing my body to hers and pushing her back onto the bed, length-wise, laying her back onto the pillows, my arms against the sides of her chest, her torso, fingers trailing down onto her hip bones and thighs, pushing her legs apart as I lift myself between them, sliding into place, we fit together so well, ball and socket.

"Are you going to come again," I ask, though it's not really a question, more a way to hear her mouth form the sounds of an answer, any answer.

"Um ... maybe ... are you going to ..." Is she really suddenly shy? She struggles to form the words. I slide my cock inside her again and she lets out her breath in a moan, a low gasp of surprise and desire.

"Yes, I'm going to give you my cock again. You can take it, I know you can. I want to see your face when you come this time." In and out of her. Sliding, rocking against her. "I want to hear you gasp against my neck. Feel the way you grip me with your legs and arms as your body opens for me. I want my mouth on you, want to taste your skin and suck the flush to the surface." Her hips roll back and let me in an inch deeper. "Ohhh yeah, that's nice, that feels so good, you feel amazing, Juliet, Juliet …"

And she's coming again, fingers clawing at my shoulder blades, my mouth against her collarbone as her skin gets supple and capillaries burst under my tongue as I make bruises on her chest, mouth open and releasing sounds of glory and awe, gasps and moans against my neck and earlobe as she tries not to thrash too hard against me. She pulls back from me hard, thrashes back against the pillows and I get this beautiful full view of her chest arching, every muscle clenched and the swell of her breasts thrust forward, nipples cherry-red against her white skin. She turns her head from side to side, arms up in angles and hands on the pillows as she calms, bends her knees tight before lengthens her legs to stretch them out, finding again the edges of her body.

I lower myself onto her again gently, soft, and she moans with the weight of me over her. I kiss her cheek, jaw, neck, and catch the beautiful scent of her lotion, whatever it is she uses, a delicate sweetness which swirls against her skin shined with just enough sweat to make it salted.

She sighs, wraps her arms around me, and looks at me, opening her eyes slow, heavy-lidded, and kisses me, mouth supple and sweet.

"Um. Wow," she says, sighing. "Spectacular." I grin, and relax into arms, so spent.

Charcoal

There is only the light scratching of my charcoal on paper. Thick and creamy, deckled edges on plyboard. Held in my lap. An indication of shadow here. Of hip, of thigh.

She's posing for me, only a black tie around her neck, black leather harness around her hips, black strap-on eagerly poised. She's draped on the white studio couch. She's calm and steady. She's watching me.

A flick of my wrist and a line for her jaw, her left breast. The angles of her come to life. I recreate her. She lets me.

I fill in details. Impressions of her, sultry, fall around me like winter is coming. I tear off another sheet and she is moving toward me, all eyes and hips, that cocky swagger.

I drop my charcoal. My fingers are blackened with it. Her lips are at my ear: "Which curves are you still missing?" She takes my hand, sets it on her hip. "This one?" On her stomach. "This?" On her thigh. "Here?"

I swallow the hesitation in my throat.

"Come on," she says. "You can do better than that." And I can. She shows me. Her tongue sketches curves and I am recreated by her from the inside when she slides.

Her lips are charcoal, and my skin is perfect paper.

The Study Date

I push her back against the door of the classroom the second she closes it, catching her jaw by surprise, my hand over her mouth. "Is this what you wanted? You want me up against you like this?"

Corinne's knees go weak and her eyes widen, looking up at me softly under her short red hair which curled around her chin in a blunt bob, the bangs across her forehead making her look like a model from the thirties. Her ivory blouse is loose and silky against her skin, a bit fallen to one side, showing the edges of a lace camisole.

I bet she's already wet.

"You've been trying to get me alone all semester. Did you think I didn't know what you wanted, when you asked me to study with you after class?" I speak softly against her neck, let her feel my breath, hot, against her skin.

Corinne can't speak. She had been taking up all the air in the room every day in our evening literature class, feisty and talkative, and I've finally caught her unprepared. I like the way she keeps glancing at me, then glancing around the room, at the windows, at the door, the small individual desk-chair sets in messy rows, as if she isn't sure she wants to be here, now that she created this situation.

"You like the way I feel, don't you?" I bring my hand to her waist, to the curve of her hip, to the front of her thighs, running it up her belly, to her breasts.

She gasps. Nods slowly. I let my fingers find the hem of her black pencil skirt and start tugging it up her thighs. She looks surprised and shifts her weight, her heels of her black pumps clicking on the hard classroom floor. She squirms and whimpers a little behind my hand. She's breathing heavier and I have to let her have her mouth again in a moment.

"Getting shy now? I thought you knew who you were playing with." Her skirt is tight and it's hard to get it to move along her legs with just one hand, I don't want to rip it or stretch it out, but I'm getting impatient. I push my hand between her thighs and spread my fingers to get her to open them, shove at the fabric. She sucks air in through my fingers, brings one hand to the wrist that is holding her mouth and the other to my shoulder, my chest, almost like she's pushing me away but she's not, she's leaning into me. She wants more.

She sets her jaw, gets her footing, spreads her legs, locks my eye contact. Getting bolder. Caught off-guard for only a moment, she's regaining that fierce self-resolve I've been fantasizing about for months: how I would unravel it, thread by thread.

I move my hand up her skirt for a surprise of my own: no panties. Her cunt is not shaven but trimmed, I can feel the soft hairs around her lips before I explore the inner contours with my fingertips. I want to plunge in. I want to catch her between my hand and the wall, feel her from inside, see how she shudders when she comes, if she can stay upright against this wall, right here.

I let up with my hand over her mouth and feather

touch my fingers to her lips, red and full, her mouth gently parted, breath sliding in and out, hot, it's getting warmer in here, I'm starting to sweat. I can feel it at the nape of my neck, on the small of my back. I'm in my favorite deep red tee shirt and broken-in jeans, but none of the windows are open and it was warm today. Temperatures are rising fast.

Her tongue is swelling in her mouth. She swallows, watches my face, I can tell my features are getting more shadowy as she's started giving over. I tease her lips with my fingertips and slide inside her mouth and her cunt at the same moment, two fingers each, she's wet and warm and strong and tight.

Shuddering just barely, she leans her shoulders against the wall and tilts her pelvis toward me, an offering.

You can have me.

I know.

Slow and deep, filling every inch as I move inside her. She opens and blooms between my hands, reaching into her as though I could pull some jewel out from her core, as if excavating a mine.

Show me those precious things you hide inside.

Corinne swells, clit and tongue; I wet my thumb to thrum against her. I'm holding her up and back with my hands, she's pressing her weight into me, opening deeper. Her desire rises and I think she's going to come, she tightens so strong around my fingers and sucks me in deep, I can barely move either hand inside her, but she doesn't, she gasps, goes limp, releases, leans her head against the wall and opens her mouth, opens her eyes, slides them sideways to look at me. Swallows a few times.

I slide my fingers out of her beautiful tight body. We both catch our breath.

I wipe my hands on my jeans and run my fingers through my hair which is falling in my eyes. She rolls her shoulders forward and her knees together shyly, then straightens up, pulls at the hem of her skirt, and takes four swift steps over to the teacher's desk in front of the chalkboard still covered with notes from our lit class and from the day's use, ghostly outlines of letters.

Her hard heels against the floor click, click, click, click, and she balances perfectly on the thin tapered heels, effortless (or so it seems to me) black straps buckling around her ankles. Much too fancy for some night university class. She regains her poise and she is all grace, all pressure and granite.

Turning to look at me, she shifts her hips side to side as she works her skirt up her thighs and bunches it around her waist, watching my face as I try not to stare, then she turns, and bends over the desk with her elbows on it.

I don't make a move. I barely breathe. I let my hungry gaze take in the curve of her ass, her pussy laid out for me, wet and open, her asshole pink, the lines of her shapely legs.

This girl knows what she wants. I love that.

She glances back over her shoulder at me hesitantly, a little shyly. I can see her wondering if she's made a mistake, been too bold, or if I'll give it to her.

Of course I will.

My brown loafers click too, but softer than hers, the leather warn down and smooth. I don't go slow this time, easily shoving three fingers into her, hard enough to tip her forward farther over the desk. Her mouth opens with a quick "ah!" but she takes it. I grip her hip and slide out easy, slick, she's so wet, so wet and easy, she guides me in and out, takes it hard, rocks against me.

In a flash she reaches down between her legs with her left hand and lays deeper onto the desk, breasts against the cool slick top of it. She lets out a moan as she flicks her clit and tightens around my fingers. I slow down, deepen, expand my fingers to fill her more. She gasps, *yeah ohhh yeah yeah* and I grin. There's that tongue of hers working again.

I've got her perfectly at hip height and wish I had a cock with me—how was I to know she'd accost me like this?—her ass is luscious and I want to take a bite of her cheek, leave a bruise, wet my fingers and work them into her ass as I plunge my cock into her cunt. Maybe she'll let me do this again. My free hand travels up, pulls her blouse free of her skirt and finds her nipples, one and then the other, smashing my hand between her and the desk as I keep thrusting and she keeps rubbing her clit, I'm closer to her and can hear her gasping, her hair is falling in her face and she is deliciously disheveled.

"Oh god, oh god," she mutters. No need to involve him, I want to reply, and bite my tongue thinking, this is the most holy thing I've done in weeks, I can feel her expanding and enlivening under my fingertips, can feel her chest sweeten and swoon as her heart beats red and strong. The buttons on her blouse are popping open and her skirt is all twisted, her hair swings next to her cheeks and ears, red as the flush on her forehead and between her legs.

I want to keep her here, poised, open, fine-tuned and sailing over waves of breath and pulse. Here, it is nothing but bliss and beauty and possibility and healing, nothing but filling the cracks and broken-down machines that are our bodies, that run us, both her and I, I'm flooded with it too, she's spilling out of herself and into me and I catch it, drink it, push myself inside her deeper to spill and capture even more. I love this part, this dance, this exchange, when we are no longer separated, one big electrical circuit, raising energy from our own bodies, flowing through us, picking up speed and momentum and density and purity as it travels between us.

But of course it doesn't last. Like all moments of

ecstasy, it is short-lived: it spills over and explodes and she comes, hard, gasping and thrusting back against me, pushing her clit so hard I can feel it inside, knees shaking, one of her feet lifting off the floor as she slides her body nearly all the way over the desk.

Her cries quiet, but I notice they bounce around the bare, hard classroom; I wonder if anyone has heard.

I've pressed hard against her as she collapsed and after a moment I disentangle, breathe, feel my own body attached to my own hand, contain myself again. She hums with pleasure and pushes herself up from the desk, pulls and twists her tight skirt back into place, sits on the desk and crosses her legs to re-button her blouse and smooth her clothes. Her ankles touch and kiss, shoes barely held onto her slender feet, just a few fine straps and buckles.

She runs her fingers through her hair, tucks it behind her ear, in a gesture so sweet I stop what I'm doing and reach for her, slide my hands around her waist and she brings her arms around my neck as we kiss, soft and sweet and slow, tender, and I realize we hadn't done this yet, am I so professional about my fucking that I don't even kiss anymore? The kissing is the best part. I sigh into it and she grins, I feel her mouth move up at the corners.

"So," she says, pulling back arms length from me, eyes sparkling. "No cock?"

I laugh, a low puff of air. "Caught me a bit unprepared, I guess."

"Mmmm." Corinne doesn't press it.

I do. "I'll bring it Wednesday. We are going to have to, you know, ahem, study, again, before the final on Monday, after all."

She's amused, still grinning. "I'll be sure to wear a skirt," she says, and kisses me again.

Fucking a Porn Star

This girl knows how to submit.

Even before I have her clothes off, even before we enter the hotel room, there is something, some coy lowering of her eyes, some demure way she keeps fluttering her wrists like dinner napkins, something in the way she purses and slowly licks her lips that makes me feel strong. Powerful. Wanted. Something that gives me permission to take.

With a girl like this, I know how to dominate.

She knows what I brought along in my carefully packed bag. We negotiated the contents precisely, both clearly able to navigate the world of online NSA personals.

My ad read: "ISO sweet, submissive girl that loves rope and flogging." The girl was the only decent reply—and the only redhead.

Once in the hotel room, lights still off, I tell her to undress (her skin revealed, pale and full of promise) then kneel in front of me. I kick my pants and briefs off, and part my slit with my fingers, standing before the girl, who begins lapping and sucking, tentatively at first, then eagerly, deeper, suckling, making small *mmm* noises like she is savoring some satisfying dessert.

The night of subtle, easy flirting at the cafe and her sweet eyes looking up at me now, mouth full, are making me so hot, and her expert tongue and pressure bring me surprisingly quickly to a thick state of desire and bliss. I came with a jerk and my hands in her hair, then reward her by nzipping my toy bag.

I take her every way I can think of: bent over the coffee table. Against the wall. Elaborately hog tied on the bed, wrists and ankles pulling each other in separate directions (that is especially lovely). Wrists tied behind her back. Fingers in her cunt, then fist in her cunt, then fingers in her ass. Beautiful.

There is something I can't pinpoint about this girl, some familiarity about the way her body shifts when she moves, the way her small, tight muscles pulse and ripple, that look in her eyes each time I turn to her, palm open, to bring a new sensation to her body. There is some way she leads me with tiny, subtle movements to know exactly what to do next. So skilled at submitting.

Hours later, we are flushed, skin shining with sweat, exhausted and still wanting each other. The hotel room is dim, only one lamp on in the corner and the nighttime city lights filtering through the curtain. The shadows are long and smoky. The bedspread, sheets, and pillows, are torn from the bed and discarded on the floor. The couch too has been attacked, pillows strewn about, even knocking over a vase that we both ignored.

My rope proved to be the favorite accessory of the evening. Wrapped around both of the girl's wrists, it is now tied to the hotel headboard, immobilizing the girl, face down, stretching her arms long above her head. Her ankles are tied, too, to the foot of the bed, but the rope has enough length that the girl can nearly raise to her hands and knees. Her ass is in the air, increasingly pink.

Raising her hand beyond her shoulder, I bring my

cupped palm down onto the flesh where ass meets thigh. A delicate sound. Precise. The girl's muscles clench gently, then release.

Again, and again, I slap and sting her ass and inner thighs, my hand hitting against her crack, swatting her clit and swollen labia, red and slick and smooth as glass, steady, and then faster, the blows coming closer together until the girl starts whimpering and straining at the ropes, inching forward to escape, and I let up, sooth my hand over her red skin and cunt, fingers exploring the crevasses of her labia and hood, slow circles, slow lazy circles around her clit, and the girl relaxes again, leans into it, moaning. Her back arches, knees and feet straining farther apart.

I pull my flogger from my bag: deerskin. Long. I drape it easily over the girl on the bed and it tickles, massages, gently caresses her skin.

Until—*thud*. I let it fall using only gravity. Again. *Thud*. A gentle sound. More like thhh. A shushing noise through the air like a librarian.

The girl arches her head back. It is a request. Four, five swats and I have my aim. Eight, nine and I have a comfortable build of pressure: each time I bring the leather down it hits a little harder, a little deeper into the muscles.

The girl squirms and writhes against the bed.

I climb between her knees and, erect, bring the flogger down again. Onto her shoulder blades. Onto her sides. Onto her ass. Finding a rhythm. One two *thud*. One two *thud*. Gathering the tails together over my shoulder, into the palm of my hand, then back down. Deliberate. Our breaths match. Gasping when the tails hit skin, moaning when they leave.

"Oh god," she whispers. "Oh god." She cringes, cries out.

"You like that?" I growl, a little harsh, acutely aware of

the ferociousness building in my stomach, under my ribcage, creeping up to my heart and throat and shoulders. I hit harder. Harder. The girl arches her back and nearly collapses on the bed.

"Relax," I whisper, caressing her skin with my palm. She crushes into the bedspread and brings her arms under her, tensing her entire body briefly before releasing, opening again, looking up at me with soft eyes. Her limbs are all sinew and bone and skin, lanky and long. She tilts her head but kept her eyes on me, responding to my soothing touch with arches of her body, breathing in. She relaxes onto the hotel sheets, then takes her arms out from their tucked position under her and bends her knees, her arms and torso laid out long on the bed, ass to ankles.

"Please, a few more?"

I grin, step off the bed behind her to get a larger swing, then tighten my grip on the flogger's thick handle and let more blows fall onto the girl's back and ass and thighs, tips of the tails snapping at her skin, not fine enough to leave individual marks but turning her entire backside darker and darker pink, in some places flushed red. She may be bruised tomorrow.

Working my entire body into the blows, I swing and hit. Swing and hit. I really am a sadist: turned on by the witness of someone else's pain. I know my cunt is wet, can feel it between my thighs. The girl moans and cringes and breathes with each contact. I work up into a wonderful beat, so satisfying, a wrist turn that looked like a baton twirl and a rhythm like timpani, steady and slow, working the flesh and bones of her, this gorgeous girl, so willing to give over, so eager to receive.

I build up speed and the girl whimpers. Harder, and she yells, pulls against the ropes, thighs cringing together. I gather my strength and let a few last blows hit.

The girl cries out with the intensity. Screams, loud then quiets.

Gently leaning into her, I float my hands above her skin as she lies still in the aftermath of the flogging, still writhing, still cringing, body melting and settling back into a new expanded shape. I softly begin moving my hands, hovering just above the skin, not touching yet and then—until—just a fingertip, just the softest brush of the pads of my fingers over the girl's smelting skin, red and stinging and sensitive to even the minute changes in the air. I set each finger, then my palm, oh so gently, barely even touching, like a paintbrush making the finest softest strokes against the exposed canvass of her back and ass and thighs.

She draws breath in hard with each brush. Arches her back. Strains against the ropes.

The reverberation of every contact ripples through her body like a firework exploding. Touching her illuminates the sensitivity, the after effects of the leather still buzzing in remembrances on her skin.

"You feel amazing," I say, completely caught up in the swirling energy between us.

She moans something, groaning, into the pillow.

"What was that?" I say, both hands on her back, leaning forward to hear her better.

"Fuck me," she says again, clearly this time, turning her head to the side, red hair falling over her face. "Please, oh god please now."

"Mmm," I agree, drawing my hands back down her body to her ass and exposed cunt, two fingers running over her lips and clit, swollen from the long night of sex, from the sensory overload, from the submission.

She moans deliciously with each touch.

I grin and keep my grip on her hip bones, sliding two fingers inside her slick cunt easily. She sighs, heavy, and opens deeper. I slide out and add another finger, a little tighter with three. She inhales and squirms a little, so eager, so open.

"Damn, that's good," I mumble, fingers sliding in and out, thumb on her hard clit. I feel her opening deeper still, pushing back onto my hand, gripping the rope that held her wrists to the headboard, rocking on her knees. I add a fourth finger.

The girl's clit swells, g-spot thickens—I can feel it from where my hand hits inside, the upper wall thick and juicy and swollen and I finger it, press against it tenderly, pet it with little laps of the pads of my four fingers.

Cries from her mouth, directly in a line connected to her cunt. Pressure here and she cries out. Pressure there and she gasps. A little harder, a little faster, and her knees shake, thighs press apart, ass presses back, back arches, head bends and her cunt opens to swallow everything, to take it all inside her, hard, to suck my hand in, to the palm. Then she bursts: it starts in her cunt and radiates out in waves, in ripples, thick quakes of bone and muscle and she makes such delicious low moans, *oh-oh-oh god, oh-oh-oh god*, and I slow, changed pressure to let up, and she folds back into herself, collapses forward on the bed, and my fingers slide out as her body calms.

I untie the ropes and we collapse together on the bed, the girl holding me close against her, sharing caresses, giggles, as we come down from our bodies' highs. We lay eye to eye on the pillows.

"You just look so familiar, I can't shake it," I say. "It's weird. We haven't met before, you're sure?"

The girl grins. "Well, I told you my name. I figured if you knew my work you'd recognize that."

I realize I can't remember it. Michelle. Marilyn. Something with an M.

She sees my hesitation and offers it again. "Madison,"

the girl says. "Madison *Young*."

"Oh," I say, and then realize: I'd just fucked a porn star.

The Pink Dress

Emily emerges from the dressing room slowly, suddenly shy, though I've seen her naked in dozens of compromised positions. She fidgets with the dress, her hair, sucks in her stomach, but her eyes are lit up and she's biting back a playful smile. She wants to wear this dress. Her inner three-year-old princess is aflame. "What do you think?" Emily asks; but the question isn't really about my preference. She wants me to want it so she has permission to wear it. Then she doesn't have to want it for herself; she is absolved of her own desires. I want her to have permission to want anything on her body that she is drawn to, regardless of its gendered implications.

I finger the skirt of the baby pink dress, its satin fabric, abundant for its near-full skirt. She looks amazing in the plunging neckline in a gentle scoop, which shows off her round breasts generously. Sleeveless, it gathers at the waist where a thick white band wraps around, tying in a ribbon at the back. She rarely finds dresses in her size; she's bigger than me, and she always complains that the selection for fat girls is really limited. It could have been a bridesmaid's dress, or a prom dress, or maybe someone's fancy party dress.

Probably custom. She's been eyeing this dress in the window display, and today was the day it came down. She asked them to set it aside for her.

"So?" She is trying so hard to be patient. The words come out in a rush. "Do you like it?"

I come up behind her as she looks in the full-length mirror barely visible behind racks of gently used clothes. I wrap my arm around her waist, not quite reaching around her but still pulling her gently back to me as she sighs, then smooths the skirt down like she's done it a dozen times before.

"I think it's perfect," I say, my lips brushing her ear. "No question."

"Really?" She's not sure I mean it, but she wants me to. "But it's so … femme."

"Yeah, it is," I say.

"But, I'm not femme!" She blurts.

"What do you mean? Of course you are," I say.

"No, I mean …" She struggles for the words. "I'm not *high* femme. I hate that term. I almost always wear jeans and tee shirts." We've been seeing each other (read: fucking) on and off for a few years, playing and going on dates. When she dresses up, she adds fancy shoes and lipstick, rarely anything more. She has some impressive lingerie, but seldom wears dresses. She wears power suits for her professional office work, where she has to keep control and is in charge of a dozen people's activities on a daily basis. She spends a lot of time looking put together, climbing the corporate ladder, and fighting the male privilege in her office, and she'd rather kick around in something comfortable and durable when she has the option.

"I know that's what you prefer, and it's perfect—your ass looks great in jeans," I counter. "Look, you're twice the femme most self-identified high femmes are. You're at home in your body, awake in your skin, not judgmental about your own waistline or anyone else's. And you have your circle of femme friends without gossip or backstabbing. If that's not high femme, I don't know what is."

"Yeah, but you have to say that."

"And I want to. I know the dress is a stretch ... but it's amazing on you. It looks like it was made for you. Doesn't it?" I ask the passing sales girl. "Doesn't it look like it was made for her?"

"It is, like, *so* cut perfectly for your body," the girl, probably barely twenty, replies. "It makes your curves look even more curvy. It's practically, like, perfect."

"Yeah. Perfect," I echo, and Emily grins at herself in the mirror.

"It is, isn't it. Yeah. Okay." She kisses my cheek and zips back into the dressing room, and buys the dress.

*

The dress-up date is my idea, and a surprise. I enlist her friend Sam, a gay boy also known as Serena, who does a fierce drag queen act and has every feminizing, over-the-top accessory one would need. We've been out drinking and galavanting dozens of nights in the past few years. Sometimes Emily and I go see him perform. Last time, he did a Judy Garland number with an incredible outfit from the forties that made him look like a black and white movie star.

"I could never do that," Emily must've whispered to me five times that night, but the spark in her eyes told me that she wanted to. I knew Sam would love to see Emily all dressed up.

And tonight, with this pink dress, he's going to help. I enlist Sam because Emily doesn't have the femme things I need, and I can't afford to buy them all. I meet Sam around the corner and pick up the fluffy underskirt that's used to puff out full skirts called a crinoline.

I knock on Emily's door, and she throws it open. "I'm here to pick up the dress," I say, after kissing her hello. She fetches it from her bedroom, still in the thrift store's lavender-colored paper bag with their logo on it, and hands it to me across the threshold.

"Thank you. Now, you remember what I told you? What's the plan?"

"First, I'm getting my nails done across the street. Then I'm going to go to Sam's at 5pm to get my hair and makeup done. Then I'll come meet you at your place, and bring the bra and panties." I know she doesn't wear the white bra and panty set with the lace trim often. I like that she saves it for me.

"What time, at my apartment?"

"Seven thirty."

"Good. Perfect. Don't be late," I add. As if she would be. She shifts her weight from foot to foot very slightly and I can see her ears beginning to flush pink.

I tuck the box with the crinoline under the arm that holds her dress in a shopping bag and draw her to me with the other, smiling as our faces get closer, drinking in her skin and hair and the sweet way her body fits.

"I won't. I promise."

"Good girl," I say, and kiss her.

*

At seven twenty-eight, she knocks on my apartment door. I greet her with more kisses and lead her into the bedroom before she sets her purse down. Some of the things are laid out on the bed: the crinoline skirt, white thigh-high stockings, a white garter belt, and her new pink dress, which I had dry cleaned and pressed just this morning. I see her hand flicker slightly as she reaches out and touch the dress, then pulls it back and makes a fist.

"Are you ready for tonight?" I take a seat in the small armchair in the corner of my bedroom and I take a sip of the glass of water I'd poured just before she arrived, with extra ice so she can hear the clink of it in the glass. She nods. Emily picks at her nails, then stops when she realizes she is probably chipping her nail polish. She must be nervous. The icy liquid is cool in my mouth and I feel it run down my throat. Her chestnut hair is mostly a silhouetted shadow, but I can see it is piled on top of her hair in spirals and curls in a way that is much more complicated than she would usually entertain. It reveals the curve of her neck, which swoops into her collarbone and, later, will lead right to her cleavage.

"Did Sam send you with jewelry?" I ask.

"Yes."

"Get it out, and put it on the top of the dresser." I cleared it in anticipation. She goes to her bag, removes a couple small boxes and a tiny clutch purse, then arranges it all so each are neat and not touching, then goes back to standing, shifting her weight from foot to foot and looking around the room.

"Take off your clothes," I say. "Slowly. Fold each piece and put them on the bed." She starts with her v-neck grey fitted girly tee shirt, quickly pulling it over her head. "I said slowly," I say, and she pauses, moves a little slower. She folds the thin fabric easily and places it on the bed, then steps out of her low, simple black flats. She pulls off her plain bra and lets her large breasts free. Her bare skin glows in the lamplight. She pulls down her tight blue jeans and steps out of them, folding them a little thoughtlessly, but I don't tell her to slow down again. She slides her plain black cotton underwear down over her legs and adds it to the pile. She fingers the worn grey tee shirt and looks at it longingly, then glances at the lingerie laid out on the bed and moves her hand to touch it, smiling as her fingertips make contact, her face relaxing.

She stands again, naked this time, crosses her arms in front of herself, then drops her arms and holds one wrist with her hand. After a moment she straightens up, and clasps her hands behind her back like she is presenting herself to me, a blank canvas. She shifts her weight again, drops her hip, but tries to stay still. She bites her lip.

"Very nice," I murmur from my corner. I uncross and recross my legs, ankle to knee, and pick up the cane from next to my chair. I can see her nipples, even in the shadows, hard and dark. "Get the bra and panties out of your bag, lay them on the bed." She does. "Now, get dressed. Start with the garter belt." She takes a breath and turns to the bed, picking it up and sliding it up her legs, securing it in place.

"Now the stockings," I say. "And the bra. Leave the panties off, for now." She dresses quickly, fumbling a little with the clasps and the delicate fabric, sitting on the side of the bed to fasten the stockings to the lace. "Now the petticoat." She looks at me a little questioning, then realizes I mean the white crinoline skirt, and pulls it in a flourish from the bed to step into it.

"The dress," I say. She pulls it over her head, evens it over the petticoat, and does her best to tie the white bow behind her back. With the extra layers under the skirt, the pink dress is even more stunning than it was in the store. "And the jewelry," I say, as she admires herself in the mirror hanging over the dresser. She takes a step closer and puts small two-stone droplet earrings in; they're delicate, just an inch or so long, hanging just enough to move when she does and sparkle when the light hits them. She reaches for the matching necklace and raises her elbows to buckle the clasp behind her neck. Her fingers tremble and it takes her three tries to hook it correctly.

Emily steps back and looks at her reflection, buzzing, hardly containing the thrill of happiness at her own reflection. Her smile is as big as I've ever seen it. She turns her head, then shakes it to see the sparkle of the earrings, tilts her chin down to see her fancy hair-do, fluffs the skirt out to the side, and finally twirls, watching the dress in the mirror and laughing, giddy.

"Come here," I say. She turns her head to me and takes short, quick steps across the room to where I am sitting next to the window in her stockinged feet. She notices the cane I have been stroking.

"Is that for me?" she asks.

"It's for your ass. For later." I set it on the table with my glass and reach out for her waist, pull her on to my lap. "Very nice," I say, stroking the skin on her arm, the the slick fabric of the top of the dress, brushing my fingers against her breasts and nipples. I offer my mouth for a kiss and she wraps her arms around my neck, opening her mouth, gently kissing back. "You look gorgeous."

"You really think so?" She bats her eyelashes. She looks like a sunrise, peeking over the horizon, breaking the dark, reaching up into the sky. She still looks like herself—just polished up a little, enhanced, prettied.

"Really. Very much." We kiss again and I get lost in her lips, her tongue, the way her hands grasp gently at my neck and shoulders. I let my hands trace her stockings, wander up under the many layers under her dress. "Do you like the crinoline?" I ask.

"Oh yes," she breathes. "Is that what Sam gave you?"

"Yes. On loan."

"It's so ... pretty."

"You're pretty, sweetheart."

She smiles shyly, kisses me again.

"Did you like getting your nails done, and your hair and make-up done?"

"Yes! It was really fun. More than I thought it would be. I thought it would be weird but it makes me feel fancy. And important. And …" She lowers her voice, her eyes a little and brings her hands up to straighten my tie, pinch my collar between her fingers. "And I knew I was doing it for you. That you would like it."

"Mmm. And you did a very good job getting all ready for me." I find the patch of skin at the top of her stockings, her sweet smooth inner thigh, and rest my hand there gently.

"I like doing what you say." It lets her mind rest, she's explained to me, and is a relief to trust enough to follow orders instead of second guessing and being in charge of everything.

"I know. And I have a few more things to do before we go to dinner. Are you ready?"

"Yes." I toss her a questioning look and she corrects herself. "Yes, sir."

"Good." I take a breath. "I'm going to warm you up for the evening. I want to give you something that will serve as a reminder that this body—" I shift my hand quickly and palm her pussy, making her gasp, then quickly attempt to maintain her composure and keep her eyes open, looking at me, "—this pretty little body of yours is mine to play with tonight."

She nods, quick, tiny movements of her head, and her eyes flicker with a hint of nervousness.

"Are you worried?"

"No, sir. I know you will take good care of me."

"That's right. Good." I move my hand away and she breathes in, her thighs quiver. I lean in to kiss her again, bring my hands to her waist and then up to cup her chin, neck, the back of her head, careful not to mess up her hair. She relaxes, her mouth softens. She tastes like cherries.

"Get up and bend over my lap. I'm going to make some marks on your ass before we go out."

She delicately places herself over me with more care than usual, though we've been in this position many times. She doesn't want to muss herself. This chair is perfect for over-the-knee spankings, with wide, low arm rests. Her stockinged tiptoes just barely reach the floor. She arches her back automatically, presenting her ass and slit to my right hand.

I caress her neck and shift my arm to cradle her collarbone and begin peeling up the layers of her pretty pink dress and petticoat. The peach of her ass is perfectly framed by her stockings and garter belt, the layers are pushed up to her hips. Softly, I bring my hand to her thighs and ass and begin caressing.

"So nice," I murmur into her ear. I start with some rapid tap-tap-taps with my fingers tight together on the sweet spots on her ass, the ones that make the flesh shake and that makes her muscles relax. She sighs, keeps breathing, keeps filling her lungs and breathing into the increasing sensation. She's done enough yoga, we've played with enough sensation play—she knows how to open.

I keep going with light taps and occasional full-handed gentle swats until I can see a pink flush starting, just a hint. She loves being hit; she snuggles down into it as if I was reading her a bedtime story. I increase my swing, raising my arm higher, and give her a few open-palmed, but not too hard yet. Her skin is fair and it is easy to leave long-lasting marks, easy to bruise and break capillaries on the surface of her skin.

Which is exactly what I want.

I continue, warming up her ass until it is bright and hot, flushed and red, beginning to show some darker parts where it will be easy to leave marks. She moans, sinking into me, humming with pleasure. When we are both warm, when my shoulder feels like it is loose and liquid and easy, I raise my arm high and let fly a few hard wallops, pausing in between, but just for a moment, to let her react. Her flesh ripples. It's easy to pound when she is thick and full like this, I don't worry so much about hurting her, or my hand. Her body shudders and I feel her tense, then relax, over my lap. I can feel the impact of my hand through her and onto my thighs, can feel her growing heat and intensity. I let my hand down again, and again, allowing gravity to pull me, sucking up the power she's handing over while I have her upturned and stunned, ready to take more.

I lean down so my mouth is by her ear again. "You are doing so well. Your ass is nice and red and starting to bruise. I'm going to get my cane out now."

She manages to move her neck slightly, twists her head and looks up at me, and nods just a little. I grip the cane from the side table and it feels hard, solid in my hand. It slices through the air with a hiss and I love the way it extends my arm. The last time we used the cane, she told me every time she sat down, she thought about what I'd done and how I'd used her. That it made her wet to have to act like she could sit normally, when really it was excruciatingly painful. That's how I want it to be tonight. Something to take away from the terror of being so femme, over the top femme, in public. Something to distract her.

The first hit with the cane is a little off, and not too hard. She gasps but does not squirm. The second is two centimeters toward her thighs and harder. Immediately a light stripe appears. She jumps a little and lets one arm drop, grabbing on to my pant leg, as she lets out her breath in a long thin stream through her teeth. The third, quicker now, is at a different angle, crossing the first two. She sucks air back in and lets out a laugh, bubbling like champagne, thrilling and tickling my nose. Good. She's warm, dropping into that blurry area past the sharp pain and into sensation.

The next dozen or so are more rapid, in succession, some lighter and some fiercely hard and biting. She takes it well. She gasps and begins squirming, but not away, not off of my lap, just to wriggle and shake off some of the building energy. I fall into a pattern of hard-hard-quick-quick-soft-caress where my eyes glaze and my cock hardens. I can see her slit becoming wet, swollen, as pink as her sweet round ass cheeks.

The striping is beautiful, thin welts rising on bull's eye circles where my hands bruised her first. I can already see some small places where my handiwork reveals itself.

I lean low against her ear again. "It's going to hurt for a while when you sit," I say, as a slide the cane away and bring my hand to her singed bottom. It is so tender and sensitive, like stretched skin over the frame of a drum, that it reverberates with every touch.

She moans. "Thank you, sir."

I bring her up onto my lap again to hold her for a minute, her ass already uncomfortable. Sitting at the restaurant is going to be excruciating. I stroke her hair and neck, offer her some water and she takes it. She snuggles against my chest, lets me sooth her, then rocks a little on my lap and I realize she is searching for my cock.

"Looking for something?" I ask.

She falters, remembers herself. "No, sir."

"Later."

She nods, tries not to look disappointed.

"I have one more thing for you, before we leave tonight. Ready?"

She nods again, brings one hand up to her mouth to bite one finger, a childish gesture of nervousness.

I almost laugh. "Nothing bad, sweet girl. This is a present. A surprise."

Her eyes light up as she slips off my lap. I go over to the closet where I stashed the bag, then sit on the bed, patting the bedspread next to me. She shuffles slowly over the thin carpet in her stockings, smoothing out the skirt of her dress and walking slowly because her legs are still weak from being bent over my lap and beaten. She brings her hands behind her, to touch her ass, as she walks, and I can tell the muscles are already sore.

I hand her the bag. She gives me a shy smile and pulls the shoe box out of the plain white shopping bag. Her eyes widen. She realizes she only brought the flat black shoes she came in.

"Oh!" She exclaims when she opens the box. They have a small strap over the arch of her foot, and a tall, thin four inch heel; it took a few days to have them dyed the exact pink shade as the dress. She pulls them both out and pushes the wrapping aside on the bed, holds them flat in her hands, grinning. "Can I?"

I slip off the bed to kneel in front of her, holding my hand out. She blushes—adorable—and hands the shoes to me, offers me her foot so I can slide them on, one at a time.

She laughs, and twirls. "I feel like these are fancy shoes from my fairy godmother, and I'm Cinderella!"

"You look amazing," I say, standing up, and offer my hands to help her stand. It may take a minute to get used to them. I take her in my arms again and she melts into me, offering her mouth for more kisses.

When I pull away I take the delicate white panties still laid out on the bed and offer them to her. "Put these on, we wouldn't want you getting your dress any more wet than it already is. Freshen up your lipstick and let's go to dinner. Are you hungry?" Her lipstick is smeared from kissing me, and she hasn't noticed. It's probably on my mouth. I quickly wipe my mouth in the bathroom mirror and when I come back in, she's sitting on the bed to step into her panties, pulling them up over her shoes and stockings, leaving them on the outside, so they can be the first thing that comes off later. She stands and picks up the tiny clutch purse she laid out on the dresser, checking her make-up in the dresser mirror. I slide my suit coat over my shoulders, watching her twist the lipstick up and pucker her lips. She would never do these things on her own, but she is flushed and giddy and thrilled, ready to go.

Emily shifts, sliding her stockings on the black faux-leather seats of my car. She is having a hard time sitting without her ass stinging. She reaches out to the dashboard and car door handle to support herself. Every time she flinches, she looks at me with those pleading, delicious wide brown eyes.

"Something bothering you?" I tease.

She blushes. "I like feeling it. Thank you, for the bruises. Sir." I'm darting in and out of lanes of traffic unnecessarily, just so I can feel the closeness of the other cars, pressing on the gears a little too hard. It is turning us both on.

We arrive at the restaurant downtown, pull into the parking lot and park right near the front. She waits while I come around and open her door, then steps aside again as I open the door to the restaurant. As soon as she enters the space she starts fidgeting. She pulls on her skirt, her coat, passes the tiny clutch purse she borrowed from Sam from hand to hand, shifts from foot to foot.

I walk up to the host at the podium. "Sexsmith; we have a reservation."

"One minute," he responds, and shifts to speak to a

server passing by. Emily's eyes are darting all around the place and she bites her lip. "Relax," I say at her ear, then louder, "May I take your coat, sweetheart?"

She nods quickly, shifts her arms so I can slide her jacket from her shoulders, revealing the dress. The pink is bright and her jewelry and makeup sparkle, drawing attention from other patrons waiting for their tables, from the host, from the server walking by. They are all wearing black. She is not used to this much attention. Immediately she stiffens, a rise of panic visible in her throat. She struggles not to cross her arms to cover herself. Her shoulders shrink.

I move to the restaurant's coat closet near the front door and hang hers up, then mine, and slip next to her to take her hand. "You look amazing," I say gently, and kiss her quickly on the cheek. She lets out a breath and nods, as if reminding herself that no one else thinks she is wearing a costume.

"Mr. Sexsmith? Right this way." The host plucks two menus from the podium and we follow him toward the back, near the big windows that look out on the street. He pulls out Emily's chair and she tries to gracefully sit, fans her skirt out, as he pushes it back in for her, already putting her courtly reception of chivalry to good practice tonight. I sit next to her, not across, at the small square table.

"Your server will be right with you."

Emily picks up the menu and begins to scan it, considering her options. Immediately someone appears to fill our water glasses and floats away; she picks hers up, takes a sip, and leaves a kiss of lipstick behind.

Immediately my dick gets hard. I shift in my seat. I love that trail of kisses her mouth leaves, love the way she works her soft inner lips over me—my hands, fingers, nipples, mouth, cunt—whatever she happens to be suckling. Her cheeks get flushed and she opens her mouth, tongue flat and soft, to look up at me. Then she sucks it all down into the back of her mouth, into her throat, and I feel her open and contract.

"Um, Sinclair?" Emily is trying to get my attention. I'm staring at her mouth, I realize. And stroking my own water glass with my fingertips, up and down. I pull my hand away and put it back into my lap, wipe my sweating palm on my pants.

"What? Yes. Sorry," I mumble.

She blushes a little, looks down with a half-smile. She can tell I'm watching her. Her hands flutter the menu closed and she releases them to her lap. I slide my hand over to her thigh. She jumps.

"Relax," I say, close to her ear. "No one can see."

"How do you know," she shoots back quietly.

"The tablecloth," I finger the satin fabric of her skirt, not quite feeling her stockings through the crinoline. My shoulders are starting to ache, ready to take her, and I shift toward her again. I reach for the hem of her dress and can just barely work my hand under it without making it look like I'm obviously reaching. Her stockings are smooth. Her legs are crossed. She uncrosses them, stockings rubbing together briefly, and parts her knees just a little. I can feel her breath on my cheek and her eyelids are getting heavy. I finger the edge of her simple white panties, then move my fingers under the elastic edge and she's wet. I can feel it.

"You like this," I accuse.

She breathes, her mouth near my ear. "Yes, sir."

"What do you like?"

"I like being all dressed up. I like how my ass hurts anytime I shift. I like how you are looking at me like a piece of cake you're going to devour. I like—oh!"

I circle her clit with my fingers. "Keep going," I say.

"I like—it's hard to be in public like this. I feel like

everyone is looking at me. I don't know what they're thinking. They might think I look silly. But I like it! I feel ... polished," she sighs, mumbling into my neck, struggling to find the words while I touch the slick folds of her pussy under the table. "I thought it would be hard, but it feels good. I guess I like it? I like it," she says again, with more conviction this time. I slip two fingers up to my knuckle into her hole and she gasps, and repeats herself, and I can't tell what she's talking about this time. "I like it."

"I like it, too," I whisper back.

The waiter arrives and we attempt to order. We wait for the food to arrive, hands above the table. It takes a painfully long time. I'm worked up after the beating, after her declarations, and I just want to fuck her. To take her, all made up, and make a mess of her. I make futile attempts to savor every exquisitely torturous moment of anticipation, but have a hard time concentrating on conversation. I have a hard time not continuing to stare at her mouth. I have a hard time not kicking my chair back and bending her over the table. I have a hard, hard time. I try not to make it obvious that I can only eat about half of my meal. It's delicious, but I barely taste it. I don't remember what I order. I try not to seem too eager when the server comes around with the check. After we get our coats, I deliberately fall back and languidly saunter to the door of the restaurant, but by the time I get to the car and my hand is back on the stick shift, my patience is out. Emily turns in her seat, her ass sore, trying to find an angle that hurts less as she watches me dart through traffic again. I can see her chest heave a little when she breathes, and her eyes are smokey, lips swollen.

She snakes her hand over to my lap and finds my cock, and her fingers are soft and lithe through my slacks. *Why'd we even go out to dinner?* I think. *I could have had her hours ago.* She's stopped shifting in her seat; whatever discomfort she was in from her beating earlier seems to be forgotten. Her fingers tap and stroke and I don't close my eyes but keep them trained on the yellow lines of the road, the other cars, the lights, taking the corners a little too sharply, very much in control.

Until we get to my apartment.

I open the door for her and she walks in first. She gives me a sly, low look like she's got my number, and I feel my knees weaken. She does, doesn't she. The insecurities about being dolled-up seem to have drained from her on the drive home. In her stance she appears to have gained an inch or two.

I wait. We both know what's coming. I feel like a runner at the starting line, energy already moving forward, holding back physically, waiting for the gun to go off. Waiting for the green light. My palms are sweating. My thighs are quivering. I am not sure how long I can hold back.

She saunters to the small table set up as a bar and pours two drinks, a vodka tonic for her and a whiskey for me, neat, no ice. She hands me the glass deliberately and our hands touch, she looks into my eyes with a smoldering glance that cuts me in half. My knees buckle and I stumble back to the wall. She takes a step toward me.

"You okay, there?"

I swallow. "Yes." I put the glass to my lips but don't drink. I feel dizzy, intoxicated already.

"Was there something that you wanted? Sir?" she adds the last word in a low, sweet voice and my cock pulses. I drop my hand holding the glass to my side. Extending her arms around my neck, she draws closer to me. I can smell the sticky sweet of her lipstick. I lick my lips. Swallow again. My mouth is dry. I lift my arm, take a swig of the whiskey, and it goes down like a knife. She offers me her lips when I drop the glass again, whispering right up next to mine but not touching. She waits. I kiss her and her mouth is like candy, like being enveloped in silk. My knees go weak again and I lean against the wall to hold myself up. Her lipstick is a smear on my mouth and I don't care. She leaves a trail of lip prints along my jaw and to the curve of my neck and I don't care. She is devouring me one kiss at a time and I don't care. My whole body shudders between her and the wall, held up by both.

She pulls on my earlobe between her lips before she whispers in my ear, "I would like to suck your cock now." It's almost a question, almost asking for permission, she knows that's usually how it works, but this time it is more of a statement of intent. I notice she doesn't say sir but I don't care. She's got me now. She drags her body down mine and her skirt fans out around her legs as she kneels in front of me. She looks up, hands on her thighs, and waits, lips parted a little, lipstick smeared and thick which makes her mouth look even more swollen. I breathe deep, trying to focus. I'm supposed to do something. I manage to set the glass of whiskey down on the side table nearby and unbuckle my belt, unzip my pants, pull out my cock. She sits up on her knees to get it lined up with her mouth.

She holds the tip of my cock right outside of her lips, breathing, looking up at me, before dropping her eyes and extending her tongue, flat and soft, to lap the underside, and brings her lips forward to circle just the head and suck. She lifts her eyes again. I swoon, my head swirling, the bowl of my pelvis full and trying not to spill over. Her tongue plays down the shaft and leisurely flicks every little ridge. Her lips are soft and warm and I can feel every contour, every smooth curve.

I lean into the wall, close my eyes, muttering, "Fuck, oh fuck." I can still feel her mouth with every brush even when my eyes are closed. She doesn't stop. When I open them again she is looking up at me, waiting, mouth poised, and then she swallows down the length of my shaft with one smooth, slow, motion, and holds me in, sliding back out as slow as she possibly can while still pressing the base of the cock against my clit. My whole body shudders, starting at my hips, extending up and down in a shockwave of pleasure.

She starts into that heavy, familiar rhythm of in and out, sliding and slick, in and out, easy and slow. I drop down into it like I was slipping into a hot pool, my body relaxing and releasing with every thrust, my attention sinking lower and lower, out of my head, into my chest, my stomach, my cunt. She wraps her hands around it, her pretty painted nails flicking along the base, curling around, pressing into me, and I rock with her, we rock together, my head bending back, hips pressing forward.

I'm going to lose it.

She grins and extends her tongue, laps and teases my cock as her hand works the shaft, then takes the whole thing in her mouth again, deep down into her throat. She pulls back and swallows the saliva gathering in her mouth, leaves her hand on my cock, still milking it, looking up at me. Her wide brown eyes are dancing, alive, sparkling, her skin shimmering with sweat that looks like glitter, the pink pink dress complimenting the flush of her skin, a little mussed but still beautiful, fancy, making her tongue on my cock look all the more dirty coming from such a good girl image.

I bend down to kiss her, her mouth a smear of lipstick, swollen and wet. My tongue slips inside and she sucks it down, too. I can feel her mouth curling into a grin while we kiss. I groan.

"Baby," I manage, a little breathless, not sure I can form words. "Fuck."

"You like that, sir? You like that from your pretty girl?"

"Yes," I breathe. "And—I want—" I stumble to my

knees, catching myself with my arms, pushing back on her and keeping our mouths connected as I bring myself to the floor on top of her.

She twists her legs out from under her and leans back, holding herself up. "What do you want?" My hands find her stockings, find the lacy tops of the thigh highs, find her garter, pull her panties down over her legs, over her shoes. They are wet, soaked through, heavy with liquid and I can smell her scent, a thick musk in my nose as I inhale. I trace my fingertips lightly, so lightly, back up her calves and knees, up her thighs, under the playful crinoline of her skirt, under the sleek layer of her dress, into the creases of her hips, onto her inner thighs.

"You," I say, pushing her legs open with my chest, lifting her knees a little as I press back into her. She lays back, lets her arms drop to the floor instead of holding herself up. I inhale the scent of her, sweet and salty, her pink lips slick and open. I barely brush my lips against her inner thighs, my eyelashes, my nose, just barely tickling, so, so soft, as light as I can manage, feeling the heat emanating from her. Little *oh*'s escape her lips, little sounds when she exhales, small snippets of pleasure as she opens up wider. She reaches down with her hands and spreads her pussy open, spreads her lips apart, pulls back the hood, and her painted nails look perfect against the pink of her cunt. I start low and slide my tongue ever so gently on the outside of her lips up to her clit, pausing to lower my mouth and suck, letting my spit get her even more wet.

Her cunt is as smooth as her dress and feels like draping silk over my lips. She moans. I repeat myself, light tongue bottom to top, this time probing just a little and suckling again when I get to her clit. Her back arches. Once more and I manage to dip my tongue into her hole and taste how wet she is. Fuck. A shiver runs through me and I notice myself grinding my hips into the carpet, tension building in my own body. She shudders and laces her fingers through my hair, pushing on my head for more pressure against her. I comply eagerly, sucking her lips into my mouth, teasing with my tongue, staying as light as I can. She presses against me more, rocks her hips up to meet my mouth, her juicy thighs crushing against mine. Her skirt twists around her as she moves and I push it back, its size in the way of me seeing her face.

I use the insides of my lips, the tender soft places, to kiss and caress. I point my tongue and flick it on her clit as fast as I can, and slide it inside as deep as I can. I suck and lick and get her juices all over my mouth. I use my nose and jaw to press against her. Then I bring one hand up and slide two fingers inside, and she tightens, gasps, immediately, I can feel it around my fingers. I gently press into her g-spot and move my fingers oh so slightly, sucking her clit into my mouth and flicking it with my tongue, and she lets go of my head and pounds her hands, pressing up into me so hard her hips come off the floor.

"Fuck—yes—don't stop—yes—" she manages to gasp. I slide my fingers just a little more, out and then deeper, keeping pressure on her g-spot, while I work my tongue as steadily and fast as I can. She lets out a deep scream and I feel her hips buck against me, shaking, pressing into my mouth and hand as her cunt squeezes tight, vibrating, that ring of muscles clamping down hard on my fingers, her stomach crunching forward as she tenses everything, everything, her thighs, her hands even, her eyes are squeezed shut, and then: she cries out again, gasping, shuddering, her body releasing, relaxing, as she falls back onto the floor. Her body curls as it quiets and she stops pulsing. She pulls me to her, up her body to kiss her, and I wipe my face on the back of my hand as I settle on top of her body and bring my mouth down to hers. She's supple and soft, joints loose as she wraps her arms around me, muscles quivering.

I hold her a while, scissor my legs around hers and curl my body against her, stroking her hair. She smooths her skirt out of the way between us and nestles into my neck, breathing quietly and deep. She's still mostly dressed, disheveled. and I want to peel her out of every layer, find her skin, hang each of these perfect items back where they are supposed to go, treat them as precious gifts.

We're quiet for a long time. "Thank you," Emily says finally. She's still fingering the hem of the dress and the seams and the details. It fits her so perfectly.

"Any time," I say back, teasing a little.

"No, I mean—really." She looks up at me and I see the vulnerability in her eyes. The femme thing—it's not usually like this between us.

"I'm glad you liked the little ... experiment," I say. "I didn't want to push too hard. You know I love your jeans and tee shirts femme, right? This wasn't about wanting you to change."

"Oh I know. And you couldn't change me anyway, not unless I wanted to. I love my look, it suits me. But, this ..." she looks down at the dress, smooths it out. "It's really special. Thanks, for giving me a place to really explore it." I finger her hair and run my fingers along her back.

I smile and pull her close. She snuggles against me, then yawns. I laugh. "Is it time for the dress to go in to the closet for a while?"

"Noooo, no, I want to wear it forever!" She sounds sleepy and so cute.

I laugh again. "You wouldn't want it to get even more wrinkled."

"I guess not," she exaggerates her pout. "Okay. Will you help?"

"Mmm yes please." I slide off the bed and offer my hand to help her up. She stands in front of me and turns around, lifting her hair off of her neck so I can unzip it. I work the zipper slowly down, and slide my hand into the dress onto her skin. She shivers. We put each item away, one by one, and return to curling up together. I'm sure we'll find another perfect time for the pink dress.

About the Author

Sinclair Sexsmith is a genderqueer kinky butch writer who teaches and performs, specializing in sexualities, genders, and relationships. Since 2006, they've written at sugarbutch.net, recognized numerous places as one of the top sex blogs. Sinclair's gender theory and queer erotica is widely published online through Autostraddle, AfterEllen, Lambda Literary Foundation, Feministing, and others, and in more than twenty anthologies, including *Take Me There: Trans and Genderqueer Erotica*, *Sometimes She Lets Me: Butch/Femme Erotica*, and multiple editions of *Best Lesbian Erotica* They edited the anthologies *Best Lesbian Erotica 2012* and *Say Please: Lesbian BDSM Erotica*, and published a novella series in 2015, which includes *Bois Will Be Bois: Butch/Butch Erotica* and *The Dyke In Psych Class: Butch/Femme Erotica*. They were awarded the National Leather Association Cynthia Slater Nonfiction Article Award in 2015.

Sinclair is a feminist Dominant, an identity theorist, a classically trained poet, and an expert in strap-ons. They live in Oakland, California with their family, and use the pronouns they/them/theirs/themself.

Gratitude

This book wouldn't have been possible without the support of Amy Butcher, all the brilliant folks in Heart Rage who share your brains with me, and my boy rife.

Thank you to those of you who read Sugarbutch: I'm ever grateful for your interaction, feedback, support, and the great conversations.

Special thanks to the patrons of Sugarbutch.net (you know who you are). You keep me motivated to write and publish. If you'd like to know more or become one of these patrons, visit patreon.com/mrsexsmith.

Thanks to the many folks who were inspiration for these stories, including: Shanna, Maya, Rachel, Madeline, Shannon, Colleen, Lady Brett Ashley, Bad Bad Girl, Jennifer, Sara Eileen, Maze, Matt, Grey, Green-Eyed Girl, Avah, blckndblue. You pushed me to write sweeter and rougher, and my work is better because of you.

Thank you to my beloveds, who are too many to list, but nevertheless essential: you keep me inspired and lit up from the inside.

Thank you to the great teachers of my life, in all many the forms in which you have appeared.